Rogue Railroad

Rogue Railroad

JOHN DYSON

A Black Horse Western

ROBERT HALE · LONDON

© John Dyson 1999
First published in Great Britain 1999

ISBN 0 7090 6343 1

Robert Hale Limited
Clerkenwell House
Clerkenwell Green
London EC1R 0HT

Photoset in North Wales by
Derek Doyle & Associates, Mold, Flintshire.
Printed and bound in Great Britain by
WBC Book Manufacturers Limited, Bridgend.

One

The muffled sound of gunpowder exploding up ahead made the tall rider rein in his hefty quarter-horse. Somebody was blasting, that was for sure. He tensed in the bentwood stirrups as the earth tremor shook them; his eyes and ears were as alert and questing as those of his wild-eyed mount. Ker-raaack! There was a secondary explosion and he saw rubble and rocks hurled skywards in a huge fountain from the centre of the ridge immediately above him.

'Git!' he shouted to his mount, dragging her head around and raking her sides with his spurs as the debris rained down upon them. If it hadn't been for the swiftness of the mare's acceleration as she spurted away, they would have been buried in a rocky grave.

'Steady, gal,' he gritted out, bringing her to a halt. The big tumbling boulders had missed them and they had been caught only by an outer hail of small stones. 'What in hell's goin' on? Looks like we've gotten ourselves into a danger zone.'

He brushed dust from his grey suit jacket, pulled his bandanna up over his mouth, waited until the black blasting cloud had settled, and nosed back towards the gaping hole in the hill. 'Why don't these bustards keep a look-out? Let's hope they've finished their shenanigans for a bit. Come on, we're gonna give 'em a piece of our mind.'

The bearded Texan in his greasy slouch hat wasn't looking for trouble. He had had enough trouble down in Mexico the past two years. There was a price on his head both there and in his own Lone Star state. That was why he had wasted no time crossing the Salt Plains, fording the Red River and heading into the Indian Territories. If he followed the Chisholm Trail north it would bring him to the Kansan cattle towns. He was intent on looking up a couple of old friends first, so had turned off into the Arbuckle Mountains in search of a route to Sulphur Springs.

He dismounted and led his horse up through the rubble of the new gap until he could see down the other side.

'I mighta known – railroad men,' he said, as he looked down at a scene of activity. A crew of pigtailed Chinese and ruddy-faced Irishmen had already raised their picks and begun to clear away the boulders. Beyond them a sturdy Katie engine, with a cow-catcher at the front and smoke idling from its tall stack, stood at the end of a single track that disappeared back into a ravine.

'Those Jaspers look like they're in charge,' the Texan muttered as he noted a haughty-looking young man in a roll-neck jersey, English-cut jodphurs and shiny riding boots, jabbing his finger at a sheaf of diagrams and discoursing with a thickset foreman or clerk-of-works in a check suit and derby hat.

They were standing beside some heavy lifting equipment and a pile of iron rails at the end of the line. The Texan reached flat ground and swung back in the saddle, anger seething in him.

'Hey,' he called. 'You durn nearly killed—'

But the men's attention had been drawn to a light-weight buggy rattling towards them along the side of the track, driven by a young woman in a high-buttoned blouse and long skirt, her hair drawn up beneath a flamboyant bonnet. She appeared equally angry, and, as she brought the buggy's high-stepper to a halt, she screamed out: 'What do you think you are doing, you fools?'

'Fools?' the young man echoed. 'Who are you calling fools? What do you want here? What are *you* doing?'

'It's that crazy woman again, Mr Casper,' the burly clerk-of-works said. 'I told you about her remonstratin' with us further back down the line. She seems to think she owns this country.'

'I don't own it. But neither do you.' The young woman brandished her whip at them as if she would like to give them a good horse-whipping. 'This is Government land and you've no right destroying it wantonly. You will have to cease this work immediately. You've already done enough damage.'

'Are you mad, woman?' Casper stroked his wavy flaxen hair back from his eyes as he studied her. 'We've sunk a lot of cash into this line and we're not stopping now.'

The girl leapt from the buggy and waved a piece of paper under his nose. 'This line must go no further until all objections have been heard in civil court.' She thrust the paper into his hand and pointed a finger at him. 'This writ has been served. You are legally bound by it.'

The Texan had eased his big liver-and-cream patch mount up closer and sat listening. She was a handsome young woman in a skinny, intense sort of way, and her cut-glass accent suggested that she hailed from Boston or some such parts. She was certainly in a lather about this.

'I've been all the way to Guthrie to secure this writ from the marshal's office. I have sent a wire to Washington about it. The land up ahead is a national heritage and must not be despoiled.'

'National heritage,' the young man muttered, his face colouring up as he studied the paper. '. . . all work on the proposed route of the Fort Arbuckle to Ardmore railroad to be suspended forthwith.'

'That's right.' She stared at him defiantly. 'It's there in black and white. Thank God I've stopped you in time.'

'Stopped us, have you? If you think we're stopping for a pile of old bones you'd better think twice.' He passed the writ to his foreman. 'Have you received this? I certainly haven't. I haven't a clue what the bitch is blabbing about.'

The foreman's rotund face split in a gappy grin as he made the motion of wiping the legal paper across his backside. A couple of rough-looking hombres with revolvers stuck in their leather belts guffawed as he ripped it into small pieces and let it flutter away on the breeze. 'Never seen it in my life, Mister Casper. What's the silly li'l cow yapperin' on for?'

'You—' the girl paled and bit her lip as if to fight back tears. 'You vandals! How dare you?' She flourished her hand at the land beyond the blasted gap. 'These hills are of highest scientific importance. My finds represent ten thousand years of history. Perhaps even more. They are unique. How can you—?'

'Shut her up, Jim. I've heard enough from the crazy blue-stocking baggage. Get her out of here. We've work to do. Tell her go look for her bones someplace else.'

'You can't be serious? You're not going to ignore the law? You can't ruin years of work?'

'Get out before you get hurt.' The young man's normally handsome features contorted into a teeth-gritted frown. 'It would not be advisable to approach the marshal again. You understand? I am thinking of your *safety*. Get out and don't come back.'

'You can't threaten me,' she protested.

'Mr Jones,' he said, wearily, 'Get rid of her.'

The burly foreman stepped forward and pushed the girl, shoving her hard in the chest; the two other men joined in, knocking her roughly back against the buggy.

The Texan sat his horse unobserved. The crowd of down-at-heel Irishmen, Chinese and other assorted immigrants who made up the railroad gang sullenly watched. The Texan frowned and reached for his lariat as the burly foreman grabbed the girl by her blouse and back-handed her across the face. 'Get lost, sister,' he snarled. 'You heard the boss.'

Jones raised his paw to give her another slap and she screamed sharply, struggling to evade him, when the rawhide noose landed over his shoulders and jerked him back. The Texan turned the mare and pranced her sideways, dragging the railroad foreman through the mud. The rope was hitched to his saddle horn, leaving his left hand to guide the reins and his right hand free.

As the foreman lost his derby hat and cursed

loudly, trying to regain his feet, the crew turned to gawp at the Texan who, in his dusty civilian suit, did not appear to be side-armed. 'What in hell are you doing?' the haughty young boss man shouted.

'I might ask the same question of you. Where I come from what you're doing jest ain't polite.' The Texan's dark eyes glinted, and there was a threat to his quiet husky drawl. He kneed the quarter-horse to one side and jerked the burly foreman off his feet again. 'It ain't none of my business, I know, but I ain't one to stand by and watch an oaf like him beat up on a lady.'

'And just who are *you* to talk to me like that? Some dirty lousy saddle tramp by the look of you.'

'Jest a stranger riding by, I guess,' the rider whispered. 'But it seems to me this lady deserves an apology.'

'An apology? She'll get no apology from me, you crazy galoot.' The young Mr Casper beckoned to the two thugs with revolvers in their belts. 'This gentleman is asking to be taught a lesson. What are you waiting for?'

Both railroadmen hauled at their revolvers, cocking them as they drew, raising them to fire. But as they did so the Texan's hand reached inside his jacket for his shoulder-hung Smith & Wesson .44 and, arm outstretched he crashed out two rounds before anyone could blink an eye. The explosions triggered the screams of the men, one with his knuckles creased, the Colt knocked spinning from his hand, the other gasping with pain and grasping his sliced forearm from which blood spouted, his revolver falling from his petrified fingers.

'That ain't advisable.' The Texan turned the S & W

on the young man whose hand was gingerly feeling for the buttoned down holster on his belt. 'Now how about that apology?'

'You'll get no apology from me. Nor will that interfering hussy. And I warn you, you'll hear more about this.'

'What are you doing, man?' The foreman had managed to struggle to his feet and pull the lasso from his shoulders. He stooped to pick up his dented derby and brushed his muddied suit. 'Don't you realize who this gentleman is? James Casper, Jr, Vice-Chairman of the Kansas-Texas Railroad Company.'

'You don't say?' The Texan spun the .44 on his finger and stuck it back inside his jacket. He began recoiling the lariat. 'Waal, to tell you the truth, he ain't no more to me than a flea on a dawg's dick. Same goes for you.' He jumped the mare forward and clouted the foreman across his stubbled chin with the side of his fist, knocking him back into the mud. 'Howdja like someone doin' it to you?'

He kneed the mare, dancing her into the dandy who scrambled back from the prancing hooves. 'Git outa my way.' He rode over to the girl, who studied him with serious grey eyes. 'You OK, miss?'

'Yes, thank you.' She touched her smarting face. 'There was really no need to intervene like that. Guns never solved anything.'

'Well they sure as dang help where I come from.'

'Hadn't somebody better do something about that man's arm? He's hurt.'

'Aw, let him bleed to death if he ain't got the sense to help himself. In my opinion, miss, you oughta do what they suggest and mosey on back to where you come from. If you like, I'll ride alongside you. I'm going that way.'

'Yes, go, the both of you,' James Casper shouted hotly. 'And take my advice, don't come back. Or else.'

The Texan gave him a scoffing grin. 'I ain't likely to. I'm choosy about the company I keep.'

The young woman climbed onto the buggy, gathered the reins and turned the high-stepping horse in a half-circle. '*I'*ll be back,' she said. 'You're not getting away with this.'

'Go to hell,' Casper yelled, as she set the buggy off at a fast trot, the stranger cantering along by her side. They passed the steam engine, its tall stack shunting smoke and its oily-faced engineer leaning from the cab, and they followed the track back out of the ravine.

'A real nice li'l filly,' the Texan drawled as he glanced across and a gust of wind caught the girl's skirt to reveal her black-stockinged calves. ''Specially when she shows her legs.'

'Don't try to be smart,' she replied, gathering the reins in one hand and smoothing her skirt down. 'I'm not in the mood.'

'I always like a Kentucky high-stepper, but they're inclined to get hot and frothy round the collar. Very temperamental.'

'Please,' she said, giving a jag of her lips as she flicked the whip over the horse's ears. 'Save me the amusing small talk.'

'Jest remarking about your hoss,' he smiled, as he rode along beside her. 'Don't take it personal. What was all that talk of bones about, anyhow?'

'I'm an archaeologist,' she gritted out, her face tense as she drove the buggy at a fast clip.

'An arky-olly—? Ain't that like an Egyptolly-gist?'

'More or less. Only not all the important finds are on the ancient sites. We have our own treasures in this country. Only men are too blind to see them. Or Philistine to care.'

'Philly-steen? Yeah, you got me there.'

'Like the high-and-mighty Mr James Casper, Jr,' she shouted out in irritation. 'All he's interested in is the almighty dollar. He's trying to ride roughshod over me. But I won't let him get away with it.'

'Them's fighting words. You mean you think you can stop that railroad?'

'I can try.'

'He'll flatten you, sister. By the look of him he ain't a man who's gonna be stopped by the discovery of a few bones.'

'A few bones?' she screeched in wonder. 'This is one of the most important finds since the tar lake of California. We're talking Mesohipous Oligocene.'

'Mesohippus—? You don't say?'

'Yes, these mountains are a window into the subterranean formations beneath us. They were originally four miles high but they have eroded until the very core of the mountain system is exposed. That is how I was lucky enough to find him.'

'Find who?'

'My mammoth. My mammoth-kill site. I've already found two projectile points in him. Spears classified as being used ten thousand years ago, if not more. I am only half-way through excavations and they want to run a railroad through me.'

A grin split the weathered face of the rider as he jogged along beside her. 'You mean there was Injins round here all them years ago? Whoo! That's kinda funny to know.'

'Well, I'm glad somebody is impressed. Not many are.' She slowed the buggy horse as the railroad came to a high-trestle bridge across a ravine and began to head down a steep trail that curved underneath. 'So long. I'm going back round the ridge. My site's south of the route they're taking. On its direct line.' She gave him a brief, helpless smile. 'I really don't know what I can do. It's too late to go back up to Guthrie to the marshal's office. Thanks for rescuing me, anyway.'

'That's me. A knight on a white charger. Well, white and brown. So, will this railroad lead me to Sulphur Springs?'

'Yes, a few miles further north.'

'Good.' He touched his hat to her. 'So long, miss.' But before he went on his way, he turned the quarter-horse back and called out, 'So, what you gonna do?'

'I said I'd fight them. And I will. They'll go through over my dead body.'

'You don't say,' he murmured and watched her go. 'Spunky li'l gal, ain't she, hoss?'

He gave a whistle of wonderment as he watched her manoeuvre the light buggy down the steep gradient, and go under the bridge and pass out of sight behind the ravine wall.

'Wherever we go there's allus somebody fightin' and feudin'. We're gonna stay out this one.' He made a kissing sound and sent the big horse forward north along the railroad track. 'I've had enough of other people's troubles.'

TWO

'Sulphur Springs', said the scrawled sign past which he ambled his quarter-horse into the small township. 'Pop. 269', had been crossed out and amended to 'Pop. 265'.

'Must have been an outbreak of fever,' he muttered. 'Maybe of the leaden kind.'

His narrowed eyes checked a hump of graveyard before he reached the houses. Four fresh mounds. Holes not dug very deep for he could see the boots sticking out of the red earth. 'Maybe that's why they call it Boot Hill.'

The township was set on either side of the railroad track which passed through a purple-walled ravine. There were a couple of heavy solid log cabins of the original Indian trading settlement, still functioning as general stores, but most of the houses and shops were of new-planed shiplap boards, unpainted, or in the process of construction. The false front of one bore a crudely painted inscription. 'Wild Cat Saloon – eats, licker, darnsin gals.'

'The sign-painter could do with a diction-ree,' he said, as he dismounted and hitched the horse to a rail alongside some others twitching in the fly-

15

buzzing heat. The big mare made the others look very inferior nags. 'I ain't gonna be long.'

From years of living out in the wide lonesome spaces he had long since gotten into the habit of explaining himself to his horse, generally the only critter around to converse with. He slid his Creedmore long-range rifle, .44–.100 calibre, out of the saddle boot. Not that he was expecting trouble; he just didn't want to lose the $200 weapon to some passer-by who might take a fancy to it. He climbed up onto the boardwalk and used it to prod open one of the batwing doors.

He stood for moments until his eyes got accustomed to the gloom, looking the place and its occupants over. He had pulled his purple polka-dot bandanna high around his throat so the vivid hanging-scar would not be seen. If there were any wanted posters pinned up, it was a scar that would surely identify him. But in the afternoon lull there was not a lot of business. A few hombres in a corner playing cards. A big-chested young pug in a natty yoked shirt, thigh-hugging jeans and Capper & Capper felt hat, leaned on the bar in conversation with the barman, who, with his beard and brawny forearms protruding from a soiled pink vest, looked more like a lumber-jack.

The Texan's sun-faded boots clomped the boards, his jinglebob spurs bouncing, alerting the man at the bar to turn and assess him as he walked across. The pug had a Hopkins & Allen .36 pig-stringed in a holster to his thigh. He gave a twitch of his broken nose. Obviously, the mud-stained, torn and crumpled cheap Spanish suit worn by the stranger did not impress him a great deal. Nor his battered slouch hat. He expressively spat a gob of brown, chawed baccy at the boards, just missing the Texan's boots.

'Yeah?' the lumberjack-barman queried.

'Whiskey,' the Texan said in a hoarse-throated whisper.

'That ain't allowed in the Nations. Doncha know that?'

'Yeah, but that don't generally make much odds. Just git it out from wherever you're hidin' it. I got a nose that can smell whiskey a mile off.'

'As long as you ain't the law.' The 'keep gave a crack-toothed grin and reached under the counter to a barrel. He filled a tumbler. 'Best homebrew. Guaranteed to rip your skull apart. Fifty cents.'

The Texan took a tentative taste, his sharp nostrils quivering, rolling the liquor round his throat. He swallowed and gave a sour grimace as it hit his stomach. 'Bit pricey, aincha?'

'Listen to him.' The broken-nosed dude swept off his hat and gave a booming laugh. 'Another tight-wad.'

The stranger's eyes glinted as he held his gaze. He turned his back to him and looked along at a bevy of females sprawled on broken chairs and a springless horsehair sofa. The oldest was of indeterminate age, yellow ringlets hanging over greasily painted features. She gave him a gappy leer. The youngest was wan, underage, in a ruffled, overlarge hand-me-down dress. She hoicked up a skinny knee to reveal her pantalettes.

'They s'posed to be the wild cats?' He struck a lucifer on his nail and lit a cheroot. 'Where the hell you git 'em? In the jungle?'

'Interested?' the barkeep asked. 'The dancing

girls come from two bits to a quarter, dependin' on your requirements.'

'What kinda dance I want to do, you mean?' He swallowed the remains of the whiskey. 'Think I'll sit this one out. Fill it up.'

'Couple more of these drinks, mister, and those gals are guaranteed to look more appetisin'.'

'Maybe.' He dug in his pocket and slapped down a handful of change. 'Maybe not.'

The barman picked out a dollar in coin and flicked a couple of pesos away. 'That greaser crap ain't accepted.'

With his over-musculated body, the younger bruiser might have been handsome if it weren't for his bent nose. He stroked back his wavy yellow hair and looked over, his blue eyes interested, but unfriendly. 'You been down Mexico way?'

'You could say.'

'What you doin' in these parts?'

'If it's any of your business, which I don't recollect it bein', I'm looking up a couple of friends.'

'Yeah, what friends?'

The tall stranger took a sip of the whiskey, more gingerly this time. 'Fella called Henry Littlejohn and his wife, Judy.'

'You mean that rat-faced Injin,' the bruiser said, 'calls hisself Howling Wolf?'

'Thass my boy. Though I don't recall his bein' rat-faced.'

'That idjit. Had to kick him outa here t'other day. He was fallin' about all over the place.'

'Rat-assed you mean? True, I remember Henry could never hold his licker. But what Injin can? It's something to do with them havin' a higher sugar content in the blood, somebody tol' me.'

'Suger content!' the man scoffed. 'He jest likes gittin' rat-faced. What that purty li'l white gal married that savage for I cain't figure. It's an insult to all decent folks.'

'Like you?'

'Yeah, like me. He should be run outa town. He's a public nuisance. One of these days somebody's gonna put air through him, an' it well might be me.'

'Yeah? That case you might have to go through me, too.'

The pug eyed him, sourly, and spat again. 'All that bull he spouts,' he growled, turning away. 'Man's been shot for less.'

The Texan looked down. The brown juice had landed closer, an inch from his boot. He took off his hat, placed it on the bar, and sighed wearily, scraping fingers through his black, steel-flecked hair. 'I'd advise you to be careful where you spit.'

'Yeah?' The big man turned to him and his thick lips spread into a grin. 'An' I'd advise you to git outa here pronto, and go join your squit-faced redskin friend.' He cleared his throat loudly, and spat a gob to splat on the stranger's trouser cuff. He patted the horn handle of his revolver and growled, 'Go on. Git.'

He obviously hadn't noticed the bulge of the Texan's revolver beneath his coat. Shoulder holsters were far from common in those parts.

'This ain't friendly.' The older man stroked his black beard, and carefully finished the drink in his right hand. His left fist flashed out, caught the bruiser by the yellow hair at the nape of his neck, and brought his head crashing down onto the bar. 'Time you learned some manners.' He pointed a finger at the 'keep who had reached to tug a wire beneath the bar. 'You keep out of this.'

The barman raised his hands and shrugged, as the big thug groaned, his hair falling over his eyes. He roared like a rutting buffalo and slammed a right at the tall Texan.

'Agh!' He groaned again as his fist contacted with hard steel. The tall man's gripped fist shot out and hit him hard to the jaw, sending the bruiser toppling back.

The younger man scowled as he supported himself on the bar. His blue eyes fanatic, he moved fast to draw his revolver. The older man was faster. He gripped the Creedmore by the barrel and swung it to crack across his adversary's head, sending him spinning and crashing into tables and chairs. As he lay there dazed a boot clamped his gun-wrist, the stranger's right hand relieved him of his revolver, and his left twisted into his blond hair, lifting and smashing his face back into the boards, up and back, up and back, until he figured he had had enough. He hoisted him to his feet, and, one hand on his collar, the other on his pants, ran him at the swing doors, sending him spinning and tumbling out into the street dust.

'Punk!' the Texan breathed out, and kicked the .36 clattering away into a corner.

'What's going on?' A beefy, balding man pushed through the swing doors. He had the tin star of town sheriff on his waistcoat, and had been alerted by the wire that ran from beneath the bar, through the wall, to a bell in his office. 'What happened to the bouncer?'

'He bounced,' the Texan said.

'And who the hell are you?'

'Nobody of any importance. You the sheriff? Good, 'cause I had a li'l fallin' out back along the trail. I'd be glad to give you my side of the story 'fore you hear a pack of damn lies.'

'A fallin' out? Who with?'

'A fella called James Casper. Him and his three flunkeys.'

'Casper?' the barman called. 'It ain't wise to tread on his toes.'

'He had his boys try to take pot shots at me. I had to dissuade them. A coupla slugs across the wrist and forearm did the trick. I ain't lookin' to kill any one. The fat fool of a foreman felt my fist. They'd been beatin' up a young lady, that's why I intervened.'

'That must be the Luffy gal,' the barman chimed in. 'She's been lookin' for trouble, too.'

'I asked you who you are, mister?' The sheriff stuck his thumbs in his gun-belt and his chest out. 'What you doing in this town?'

'Law abidin' citizen. Visitin' friends. The handle's Jedediah Timms.' The Texan gave the name of a former Ranger friend, and lied, amiably, 'I'm in cattle. Got a spread down on the Mex border. Headin' north to Abilene. Lookin' to do business in that town.'

'Yeah?' The sheriff had an exasperated look, his too-tight shirt bursting its buttons, a stubby tie knotted crookedly beneath his double chin. 'If I was you, stranger, I wouldn't bother visitin' no friends. Take my advice, git on your bronc, and jest keep goin' out of this town as fast as you can if you want to stay healthy. You get me? Casper ain't the person you want to tangle with.'

'He might frighten you, Sheriff,' the Texan grinned, picking up his rifle, and pulling down the snap brim of his city hat, 'but he don't me. Been a long time since I seen my friends. I'm gonna spend coupla days with 'em, and then be on my way.'

'Who are they?'

'Thet Injin-lovin' bitch, Judy Littlejohn,' the barman growled from behind his bar.

The sheriff eyed the Texan uneasily. He had the feeling he had seen his lean, bearded face in a mug-shot some place. He needed to go back to his office to check him out. He followed the tall stranger as he strolled through the batwing doors back out onto the sidewalk. The blond-haired bouncer was dunking his head in a horse trough, wiping the blood from his face. He scowled, and watched them, menacingly.

'Well, it sure was time someone give that swaggering bully, Bret Spalding, a thrashing,' the sheriff muttered. 'My name's Hank Lipcott. If you ain't gonna take my advice you'd better watch your back. We buried four men who argued with Casper only the other day.'

'Yeah? Ain't you supposed to be the law?'

'What can I do? I'm only one man.' The sheriff jerked at his tie as if it were choking him, and walked off towards his office. 'You'll find young Littlejohn along at the soddy school,' he called back.

Three

'Sink me! Shiver my timbers! And other exclamations of nautical surprise. It can't be?' The young Wichita stood with chalk in hand before the blackboard as the tall black-bearded Texan stooped his head to step through the door of the square schoolhouse built of turves. 'It is! My old *compadre*, himself, Black Pete Bowen. Children, you may take a break. In fact, you can go home early. I may well be due to celebrate. I might even be inebriate.'

'Not so much of the Black Pete,' the Texan gritted out. 'The moniker's Jedediah Timms in this town.'

'Jedediah! I like it. Inspired!' The Wichita's handsome bronzed face split into a wide smile as he put both arms round Pete and bear-hugged him. 'You old sonuvagun. Don't tell me you're still on the wanted list? A little bird told me you'd married and settled in Mexico with your own silver mine.'

'Thangs didn't quite work out. A fella called Ramón Corral, the Mexican Vice-President, decided he wanted the mine and my wife. I had to leave that unfortunate country in a hurry.[1]

[1] See *Bad Day in San Juan*

23

'Not before you gave 'em a run for their money, I'm pretty sure of that.'

The Indian children stood grnning up at them as they ceased hugging and punching at each other. 'Boys and girls, meet my blood brother, one of the finest honorary warriors of the Wichita tribe. What was it the Cherokee called you in the war – Black Pit?'

'That's our secret, kids,' Pete grinned at them, pulling some change from his pocket and showering them with it. 'I don't like to brag about it. Go buy yourselves some candy.'

'School may be closed tomorrow,' Henry called after them. 'We've got a lot to talk about.' He turned to rub out some odd squiggles on the board.

'What's that. You ain't teaching 'em Cherokee?'

'What me, sir? No, sir,' Henry howled. 'This is the Chickasaw Nation so I have invented a Chickasaw alphabet. Or re-invented it, perhaps. Like Cherokee it has much in common with the Greek alphabet, according to signs I have discovered on cave walls. This reaffirms my contention that my people, the southern Indians, did not come from Mongolia across the Bering isthmus, when it existed, but by boat, or raft from the Mediterranean. They made landfall in southern Mexico and spread northwards. We may well have come from the sunken city of Atlantis.'

'You don't say? Looks like us whiteys got it wrong. What's more important is, where do we get our hands on a jug of whiskey in this dry country?'

'Aha, never fear, *amigo.* I have my own still out in the woods near the farm. Better than that rotgut they sell in the saloon.'

'It sure couldn't be worse,' the Texan agreed, his

head already beginning to buzz. 'So, how's life with you, Henry?'

'Mighty fine,' the Indian grinned, pulling on his fringed buckskin jacket and his tall black hat, 'as you Texans say. You'll see. Judy is a tophole squaw. We have two little ones now, a boy and a girl.'

'Lead on, McDuff. That your pony I saw outside?'

'Sure thing.'

'I can't believe it's five years you've been gone, Pete,' Judy said. She was holding her baby boy to her breast, and the little blonde girl, Bess sat on Howling Wolf's knee.

'And you don't look a day older,' the Texan grinned. 'Bess is gonna be a little bobbydazzler like you. She's got your gold curls.'

'Yes, that is odd, isn't it?' A beaded band held back Howling Wolf's shoulder-length raven-black hair. 'But, perhaps it is not a bad thing. She will have more of a chance to compete in the white world.'

'What made you leave Lodgepole Creek and come south?'

'I wanted to be nearer the Wichita sacred mountains.'

'Henry wasn't cut out for digging down in that coal mine. We sold it. Got a good price. We gave half to Daddy. But you know what he was like. He caught a riverboat down to Nawleans and spent it all in the casinos. He died of drink, gambling, and wimmin.'

'Sounds like he died happy.'

'Things were good here,' Howling Wolf said. 'Until the railroad. Now bad people, bad things happening.'

'Yeah, so I've noticed. I came across a creep called

Casper putting the muscle onto some gal who's got objections to his railroad.'

'Miss Luffy?' Judy exclaimed. 'She's a real nice lady. Did she get hurt? Is she OK?'

'Her feathers were a bit ruffled. I saw her on her way. One determined li'l party.'

'Oh, yes,' Howling Wolf said, suspiciously. 'This old dog's only been here a day and already he's sniffin' round her skirts. He always did like the thoroughbred fillies. That lady's got a lot of class and a fine brain, full of many interesting things.'

'She'd suit you, Pete,' Judy smiled.

'Not me,' Pete protested. 'I ain't interested. God protect me from another blue-stocking. Now where's that jug you're hidin'?'

The Texan woke up sprawled in the hay of the stable beside his quarter-horse, which was busy chomping at a bucket of oats. His head was pounding like a Cheyenne war drum, and he had vague memories of yelling, singing, dancing, and stumbling about under the effects of the sourmash.

Judy was tugging at his sleeve. 'Here, drink this,' she said. 'A nice cup of coffee to do your head good.'

Pete groaned and eased himself up on one elbow. 'Where am I?'

'We ain't got room in the cabin for another bed so Howlin' tossed you in here.' She wrinkled her nose. 'Phew! You whiff like a worn-out hoss. What you need's a hot tub. I'll git the boiler stoked up. What you wearin' this cheap ole summer suit for?'

'I crossed the Rio Grande in a kinda hurry. It was what I was wearing at the time. To tell you the truth I'm down to my last few dollars. So, I guess, honey, I gotta be headin' on. I need to get to Kansas and rustle up some finance.'

'You ain't changed much, have you? I s'pose that means hittin' a bank?'

'Waal,' he said, taking a sip of the steaming coffee. 'They can afford it. And they ain't likely to lend me none.'

'You gonna be a rolling stone all your life?'

'Honey, I was happy for two years down in San Juan with my mine and my wife until Corral and his murderers rode in. Same thing with my ranch and first wife, Louisa, down in Texas 'fore the Murchisons burned us out. It seems like I ain't never gonna get no peace.'

'You're gittin' too old for bank-robbin', Pete.'

'Sure, I know. I'm gonna get me a stake and head north to Montana where nobody knows me, try homesteadin' again. I ain't an outlaw by choice, Judy.'

The girl knelt beside him and smiled, wistfully. 'Funny, isn't it? That first time we met. We woke up next mornin' in a barn like this.'

'Yeah,' he grinned, ruefully. 'And it's a good job I'm a gentleman or you might have been put on the rocky path of sin.'

'Come on, you ole whiskey-breath. There's ham, eggs, waffles, hot biscuits and honey for breakfast. That suit you?'

He grimaced, holding his sourmashed guts. 'Think I'll jest stick with coffee, if thass OK by you.'

He was luxuriating in a barrel of hot suds, smoking a cheroot, and feeling more civilized, when Judy came into the parlour with some clothing over her arm.

'Here,' she called, cheerfully. 'This is Daddy's Sunday suit, hardly been worn, and one of his shirts and vests. Might fit you. He was short but sturdy, 'bout the same shoulder size. Winter comin' on soon, you need something warm to wear.'

'Aw, that would be too small for me.'

'You'll have to try.' She picked up his duds, fastidiously, and dropped them in the stove top. 'You ain't got nuthin' else now.'

'Hey!' He got to stand up in the tub but hesitated out of modesty. 'What you doin'?'

'Whoo!' She stared at the knotted, intertwined scars on his back. 'How the hell you get that?'

'A whip-lashing Corral gave me to remember him by. He likes his boys to cut to the bone.' The Texan couldn't help a shudder going through him as it came back to him. The whistle of the lash cutting deep, but he sat down in the water, grinned recklessly, and raised a fist to her with the missing middle finger. 'Thass the one I lost when your daddy saved my life. Cain't give you the finger sign no more.'

'You just try these on and behave yourself. I gotta go see to the kids.'

Pete did so, drying himself off and pulling on the underwear. It was clean and warm. The flannel shirt and suit jacket, of thick grey homespun, fitted fine. But the pants were a problem. They ended abruptly half-way up his calves.

'Holy Jehosaphat, just look at him!' Howling Wolf crowed. 'Them white hairy legs. You ever seen such a sight?'

'Don't put him off. Pete can't help being a long-shanks.' Judy covered her mouth and her own gulps of laughter as she came bustling in. 'I'll soon extend

the legs from an old pair of pants. Or he can tuck
'em into his boots.'

'I guess,' Pete said, accentuating his bandiness,
'I'm in your hands.'

'What we gonna do today?' Henry asked, after he
had finished his chores out in the stables and corral.
'I had an idea it might be interestin' if we rode over
to see that Lucy Luffy gal at her dig site. She's
unearthed some dang great mammoth tusks.'

Pete was pulling on his trousers with their different coloured leg-bottoms. He gave a jag back of his
lips, doubtfully. 'I dunno. I was thinkin' of moseying
on.'

'Aw, come on. You can't go just yet. You've got to
stay another day or two, *compadre*. Might never see
you again.'

'Waal?' Something stirred in his chest at the
thought of the sparky archaeology girl. That old urge
a man could never escape from – no matter, it
seemed, how old he got, or how many setbacks he
had. He smiled, slowly. 'Maybe we could.'

Judy, though, looked anxious, brushing a coil of
her corn-coloured hair from her eyes as she put her
sewing kit away. 'I'm not sure that's such a good idea.
Maybe Pete should be on his way.'

'Come on, honey. We can all go in the wagon. It's
only a three-hour drive,' Howling Wolf yelled. 'I want
to see how she's progressing with those finds.'

'Henry, there's me and the kids to think of. You
ain't got no criminal record for them other things
you two did, I mean, like robbin' the train.'

'Yes, that was funny, wasn't it? They actually gave

me a reward for finding the stolen loot. White man's real crazy.*

'Pete,' Judy cried, sharply. 'You're not gonna go gettin' him into any trouble, are you?'

'Who me? No, don't you worry, honey. We'll just go take a look-see.'

'I'm not so sure,' she said, glumly, wiping the baby's nose. 'Trouble seems to surely follow you wherever you go.'

'Not no more. I ain't gettin' involved in other folks' affairs.'

'There, you see?' Henry said. 'And I ain't gonna help him, even if he does.'

* See *The Train Robbers*

Four

'There she is,' Judy called, as they left the cabin and walked over to the corral. 'Your old grey mare.'

'Well, I'll be a blue-assed baboon. It is, too.' The mare pounded across and gave a shrill whinny of greeting. 'I do believe she remembers me. Hiyah, gal!'

He had raised her from a foal, and had left her with them when she herself was carrying. The father had been his black stallion, Jesus, who had been shot from under him in Mexico. He fondled her head, and she seemed to recognize his voice. 'You must be about twelve years old now. Who's this one by her side?'

'This is her son, Rudy,' Howling Wolf said, throwing a braidgrass rope over the neck of a feisty four-year-old. 'He goes like the wind, doncha, boy?'

'Looks more like an Appaloosa. Those black spots on grey. Fine animal. I shoulda been a horse-breeder. But I can see who's hoss he is.'

The colt was nuzzling Howling Wolf's nose. 'No, my friend, he is yours by right,' the Indian said.

'You've fed him, broke him. I ain't come to take him away. He's yours.'

'I didn't break him, I bond with him.' Henry was

obviously pleased he wouldn't lose Rudy. 'We Wichita don't break a horse's spirit like the white man does.'

They put the grey mare in the shafts of a light flatbed wagon, Judy taking the reins, Bess snuggled in beside her on the box, the baby trussed in a papoose-board hooked beneath the seat and swinging to the motion as they rode.

They did not go into Sulphur Springs but turned off, following the railroad until they reached the trail that wound down under the pine trestling, and set off through the granite hills, which were smothered with a mantle of green and yellow summer flowers, through which long layers of exposed rock broke through. The September sun shone down from a clear blue sky and the three friends sang merrily as they went jangling along.

'I was a good li'l gal 'fore I met you,' Pete warbled, in his cracked baritone, as Howling Wolf wailed a chorus. 'You put my head in a whirl, what can I do?' He burst out laughing. 'Ain't it odd how these stoopid songs stick in your head?'

They paused for lunch by the clear pool of a natural spring that came bounding down the hillside in a series of small waterfalls, and watched a dipper flitting from rock to rock as it plunged into the flow. Judy brewed up a canteen of tea which she doctored with herbs and passed around. 'It'll be good for your hangover,' she said.

'I'd rather have whiskey,' Howling Wolf grumbled, but knew he wouldn't be allowed any more for a while yet. He sat cross-legged and sharpened greasewood arrows for his yew bow, which he carried on his back. His old Dragoon six-shooter was lodged in his belt.

'You partied last night,' Judy said, as she sat in her long cotton dress, and straw hat. 'You gotta behave yourself. You both gotta behave yourselves.'

'We sure gonna do that,' Pete drawled. 'Doncha worry none.'

The site of the archaeological dig was more extensive than he had anticipated. It had been dug deep into a steep-walled ravine that cut through the hills in a north–south direction, so he could see why the railroad wanted to go through. There was a makeshift cabin, some tents, and about twenty men, mainly Indians and Chinese coolies, down on their knees carefully scraping soil or carting it away.

Among them the Texan caught sight of the girl, wearing her white blouse and ankle-length skirt, her hair coiled up on top of her head. She had a pad on one arm, upon which she was making notes, and sketching in pencil. Below her in a trench was what appeared to be the exposed rib cage of some huge creature. She was so engrossed in her task she hardly noticed their approach.

Nearby, sitting at a camp table, was an elderly man, with a grey goatee beard, in spectacles, wearing a solar topee, and safari clothes. He had a very professorial air, and he, too, was busy, examining beneath a magnifying glass what appeared to be flint lance-blades and taking measurements.

'How!' Howling Wolf called. 'Miss Luffy, how's it goin'?'

She looked up, surprised, and seemed not exactly pleased when she saw the tall Texan. She made a downturned grimace of her lips. 'What are you doing here?' she asked, in a none too friendly manner.

'Jest payin' a social call,' he said, stepping down from his horse.

'Mind where you're stepping. And keep that wagon back over behind the tents.' Miss Luffy brushed a strand of hair from her eyes irritably, loath to be interrupted, and went on with her scribbling.

'What's that thang down there?'

'That is a mammoth. Its great curled tusks are over in those crates awaiting transportation. This is a very important find.'

'Yeah, so you said. So this critter used to roam around these parts, huh?'

'Yes, along with the camel, ground sloth, long-legged bear, and a very small form of horse – before they became extinct.'

'You sayin' the Injins used to kill these durn great critters?'

'Yes. They would drive them into pits. Or kill them with wooden lances. We have found three large projectile points embedded in the carcase.'

'You don't say.'

'I do say.' She looked up and her sage-grey eyes met his, but recoiled at the intensity of his dark regard. She looked away, faintly embarrassed. 'My colleague, Dr Hyram Stares, is cataloguing them at this moment.' She led him across to the table. 'Professor Stares, this is ... I didn't catch your name?'

'Jed Tibbs – I mean, Timms.' When she eyed him, curiously, he laughed, 'I sometimes forget my name.'

'Wow!' Henry whistled. 'Can I take a look at that?'

'Be very careful,' Dr Stares emphasized, handing one of the points to him between two fingers. 'It's very strong – it's lasted twelve thousand years – but at the same time it's as delicate as it is precious.'

'Look at the fluting of that lance-head,' Howling Wolf whispered with awe. 'Look at that razor-sharp edge and point.'

'Look at that hole drilled almost all the way into that thin winged bannerstone,' the professor said. 'It's a gem to behold. You must remember they did not have our modern tools.'

'These people were not savages, as they are so often depicted,' Lucy Luffy put in. 'They had a highly skilled culture. We have found some beautifully designed pottery. In my opinion they were as intelligent as we are today.'

'Maybe more so,' Pete grunted, 'when I think of some of the lunkheads I've met.'

'Quite.' She met his eyes again and allowed him a brief, tight-lipped smile. 'Hello, Mrs Littlejohn. How nice to see you. Would you like to put the baby in the shade of the tent? Can I offer you some refreshment'

She seemed to have resigned herself to the interruption and led them over to a tent-cookhouse where a beaming Chinese was busy preparing the evening meal.

'Coffee? Biscuits? Take a pew.'

They squatted around on camp chairs and boxes as Henry peppered her with questions about where the finds would be taken to. 'I think they should stay in Indian territory. We could get a grant to build our own museum in Sulphur Springs.I could be the curator.'

'The main task is to get them to safety. I sympathize with your ideas, Henry, but the professor and I both feel these discoveries are of such importance they should go to the museum in New York.'

'Yes, but they were our ancestors. It's our heritage you are stealing.'

'If we could be sure they would be safe, maybe,' Miss Luffy replied, as the others looked a tad uncomfortable. 'But nothing appears to be safe in this wild western country, not even, if I may be so blunt, your own people's future.'

'That's true,' Henry said, sullenly. 'White men are all thieves.'

'What are you doing about the railroad?' Pete asked.

'What can we do? I obtained an order for them to cease work, which, as you saw, they flouted. I have telegraphed the marshal's office at Guthrie asking for immediate assistance; I've even appealed to Washington, but I fear we may be too late. It is useless expecting the sheriff at Sulphur Springs to do anything. These railroad people think that they have a divine right to run roughshod over all in front of them.'

'If the Government gave them these land rights before you found this ... this mammoth, then I guess you've a problem. The railroad's obviously ploughed in a lot of money on this run and they ain't likely to stop.'

'Whose side you on, Pete?' Judy asked.

'I'm jest facing facts. There's only one thing'll stop 'em – force. And that you ain't got.'

'Alas no; nor do we want a fight. That's why we want to get what we can crated up and moved out before they come. We may be forced to abandon the rest, I hate to say.'

'This is terrible!' Henry cried. 'Can't we do anything about it, Pete?'

'Nope. I ain't fighting for a few bones,' he growled, as he accepted a cup of coffee from her. 'I'm goin' to Kansas. Anyway, the odds is too high. Me against how many?'

'Very sensible, mister . . . I thought you said your name was Jed.'

'Oh, I been christened quite a few names.'

'Well, Jed or Pete, I've told you before, I abhor violence.'

'Me, too,' he said, and bit into a biscuit.

'Is that the latest fashion?' She gave a catlike smile eyeing his trousers, one cuff brown, the other blue.

'Make do and mend,' he said, surlily. 'That's the way it is out here.'

Henry wanted to engage her in conversation about the runestones found in the Territory which scholars claimed testified to the visit there by descendants of a Viking, Eric the Red, in AD 900. 'Why!' he shouted to the cook, 'Chinese monks came here years before the Europeans. A carved statuette of Shu Shing Lao, the Chinese god of longevity has been found here. That kind of wood has been extinct for hundreds of years and dates the visit to before AD 500. Christopher Columbus was a nobody.'

'Yea,' the cook grinned back. 'Tha' not surprise me.'

'I would love to stay and talk,' the girl said, touching her nose with a dainty forefinger, 'but we are terrible busy.'

'Sure,' Pete drawled, getting to his feet. 'It's been very interestin'. Nice to see ya 'gain.'

His dark eyes knitted together as he stopped to listen. There was a yip-yip-yippin' sound. Men's voices making Comanche yells. A tattoo of hooves on the hard ground.

'What in hell?' Pete put his arm out to Judy. 'Get
them kids and get your heads down.' He ducked
under the tent flap and saw them coming, twenty
riders on wild, leaping mustangs, ploughing down
the hillside and along the ravine bottom, the sound
of their six-guns reverberating off the cliff walls. He
heard the snarl of a bullet and the Chinese cook
behind him shriek as it cut into him. The cook
hung on to the Texan as he crumpled down. Pete
laid him aside and reached for his Smith & Wesson,
raising it to send the leading rider spinning into
eternity.

'Jeez,' he whispered. 'The dingbats. What they
playin' at?'

Professor Stares rose from his table to his feet,
blinking with puzzlement and fear through his spectacles as the armed riders came thundering towards
him. One wearing a tall Capper & Capper, and a long
white duster, reared his mount up over him, and
fired point blank with his revolver. The professor
raised his arms, pleadingly, and fell back. The
gunman was masked with a black bandanna, but Pete
glimpsed yellow hair at the nape and saw his thick
physique.

'That bastard,' he gritted out, and snapped off a
shot his way. But the mustang whirled, and the shot
went wide.

Howling Wolf was by his side, his Dragoon kicking
in a two-hand grip, firing at the marauders as they
went galloping by, and two of them paid the price at
his hands.

Pandemonium reigned as the unarmed Indian
and Chinese workers tried to escape from under the
horses' hooves, screaming and shouting, running

hither and thither, as the men sent them rolling like
potted jack rabbits.

The slim girl, Miss Luffy, was trying to push past
him out of the tent door, but Pete gripped her by the
waist and held her back, firing as he did so.

'What you doing?' he shouted, as she struggled
with him. 'You trying to get killed, too?'

She looked up at him, her thin face aghast. 'Let
me go. We've got to stop them.'

He held on tighter, as his self-cocker double-action
gave an ominous click. He was out of lead. The girl
met his eyes, her bosom pressed close to him, and,
for moments, it was as if there was more than anger
and fear of these men in her eyes.

'Get back in the tent,' he shouted, thrusting her
away. 'Stay down.' And he bent low, sprinting towards
his horse through the hissing lead.

The *renegados* had gone ploughing through the
ravine, trampling on the carefully exposed trenches,
chasing the workers away up the hillsides, sending
lead about their ears from their revolvers and
carbines. But many of them, too, were out of ammunition, and pausing to reload.

Pete didn't give them time to prepare themselves.
He leaped onto the liver-and-cream quarter-horse,
jerked the Creedmore out of the boot, caught the
reins between his teeth as he gave a shrill rebel yell,
and set the horse speeding towards them, levering
the rifle as he rode, and cutting four more men from
their saddles as he tore through them. They
succumbed with surprised groans of agony as his lead
thudded into their chests.

But they were hard men and, in spite of their
losses, they still had the advantage of numbers as they

lined up to face him. The Texan hauled in, swirling
the big horse around, and prepared to charge once
more. He guessed he had another six slugs left in the
magazine. He narrowed his eyes, and gritted his
teeth, as his adversaries sent a hail of lead his way, a
slug ripping through the shoulder of his new jacket.

Suddenly, however, one of the men facing him
threw up his arms and toppled to one side of his
horse. Pete saw an arrow in his back. Another man
screamed, as he turned to see what was going on, and
the greasewood pierced clean through his throat.
The others hauled around their horses in confusion,
not knowing whether to protect their front or their
rear, as Henry's arrows and Pete's bullets hammered
into them.

'Come on!' the masked rider in the duster roared.
'Less git outa here.'

Howling Wolf had concealed himself among some
boxes, and continued to fire his bow as fast as they
could their revolvers. The marauders went leaping
over him. Yet another white man bit the dust, but
went bumping away as his boots caught in his stirrup.

As the men charged down the ravine, back the way
they had come, Pete galloped after them, firing his
Creedmore until all his bullets had gone. He reined
in and watched them go. Then he walked his horse
back towards the ravaged camp, the fire of battle still
in his veins, angry and disconsolate both.

'Watch out!' Miss Luffy called from the doorway of
the tent and pointed to one of the wounded
hombres who was raising himself and aiming his gun
at the Texan. Pete hurled his empty rifle at him, and
swung from the saddle, as the man's lead took off his
hat. He pulled his Bowie, grabbed him by the throat,

and plunged the blade into his heart.

'Oh, my God,' the young woman cried, a sob in her throat, as she watched him calmly let the man sink away, wipe the blood from the knife on the fellow's coat, and re-sheath it as he stood tall. 'How *can* you?'

'How can I what?' he asked, genuinely perplexed.

'So cold-bloodedly, all this.' She waved her arms vaguely at the scattered corpses, at the groaning wounded. 'It's horrible.'

'It was them,' he said, 'or us.'

Five

Howling Wolf was doing a war-dance and waving a bloody scalp in his hand – the hair of one of the men killed by his arrows.

'Hey, Henry, that's no way to behave. You're supposed to be civilized. We didn't send you to that college in the East for this.'

Howling Wolf whooped and danced some more, triumphant. 'I been longing to do this for years,' he yelled. 'Revenge on the white man is more than sweet.'

'Yeah, well, killin' 'em's one thing. Scalpin's another.'

'Look what you've done, Pete,' Judy cried. 'Death seems to follow you like a black cloud. I knew we shouldn't have come here.'

'Hey, hold on. I didn't start this.

'Well, it does. How many men did you kill down in Mexico?'

'God only knows. I guess about thirty in the same number of minutes to fight my way out of Corral's hands. They were scum, hired killers, same as these.'

He reloaded his weapons, squinting along the sights of the revolver, clacking the new swing-out cylinder home. Judy looked around with dismay at the invader's bodies, counting to twelve.

'So what does that make you.' Lucy Luffy's haughty voice asked. 'Aren't you just another killer, yourself?'

'Maybe it's as well I am,' he growled, raising a dark eyebrow at her. 'Or you might not be around. You'd be lying dead beside the professor there. You don't think they would have spared you?'

'Oh, poor Dr Stares,' she said. 'A find mind, a great brain, cut down by this squalid worship of mammon.'

'You were warned. This man Casper appears to be ready to stop at nothin'. The sooner you get back to your books and bones and museums in the East the safer you'll be. It's these poor damn Chinks and Indians I feel sorry for. They weren't hurting nobody. There's half a dozen of 'em dead, and a couple half-dead by the looks of it.'

'My poor cook, too. He was the first to go.'

'He won't be makin' no more chop suey,' Pete said, rolling him over with his boot. 'We got a pile of buryin' to do.'

'Somebody's got to pay for this,' Howling Wolf shouted. 'I want vengeance for my people. I say we go get the top man.'

'No, Henry, please.' Judy hung onto his arm. 'Don't get involved. They'll kill you.'

'I am already involved. What do you say, Pete? Are you going to take this?'

The Texan shrugged, his face in a melancholy set. 'It ain't none of my business.'

'Look what they done to your site, Miss Luffy,' the Wichita shouted. 'You gonna turn tail, go back East? You gonna let them win, drive their damn railroad through it? Why don't you ask Mr Bowen to help you?'

'Vengeance? Killing? What is the point of it?' she cried. 'I hate all this.'

'Looks like them Philly-steens you spoke about is goin' to win after all.' The Texan strode away to look at one of the injured gunmen, who was holding a hand to his side and groaning, piteously. 'For Christ's sake, shuddup. Or do you want me to finish you? Who sent you? Casper?'

The man screwed up his eyes with pain and nodded. 'I guess.'

'Get up.'

'What?'

'Get up. I ain't no doctor.' He began to haul him to his feet. The man stood swaying, looking at the blood seeping from his side. 'Henry, give me a hand to put him on a horse.'

'What are you doing? That man's in no state to ride.'

'He's got two chances. That's more than they would have given us.' With Howling Wolf's help he pitched him into the saddle where he hung over the horse's neck. The Texan took a lariat and tied the man's boots to the stirrups and his wrists beneath the horse's jaw. 'You can tell Casper we're coming in, but we ain't lookin' for trouble. The lady's pulling out.'

'Wait a minute,' she snapped. 'No! No, I'm not . . . I'm not giving up my work. You can tell him I would rather die.'

'Yeah? She's changed the message. You heard. So git.' He slapped the horse on the rear and it went pounding away back towards Sulphur Springs.

'Thank Gawd he's gone. All that groanin' was

gittin' on my nerves.' The Texan turned away to the tent. 'You got a spade? And some vinegar?'

'How much do you charge?' she called.

Pete paused and looked back at her. 'What did you say?'

'What is your fee? You're a professional gunman, aren't you? At least, you seem to be.'

A smile spread across his face. 'Lady, you couldn't afford me. Not at these odds.'

'I've got funds. Name your price.'

He scratched his beard, his dark eyes amused. 'A thousand dollars.'

'That much?' Miss Luffy gave a gulp of surprise. 'But most of his men are dead.' She waved her hand. 'You've just killed twelve.'

'He'll get more. And I figure they won't be amateurs next time. That's my price. Take it or leave it.'

'You can have me for free,' Howling Wolf said. 'I will be proud to help you.'

'No,' Judy cried. 'Please, no.'

'Not you, Henry,' the young woman said. 'I'll just have him.'

'Yeah, go home, Howlin'. Keep your head down.'

'Don't worry,' Miss Luffy said to the Texan. 'I can get the funds.'

'You better.' He put out a hand to shake on it. 'This ain't a job I'm lookin' forward to. But I'll do what I can.'

He fetched the spade, vinegar and some brown paper, and went to an Indian who was stoically examining a bullet hole in his thigh. 'Here,' he said, soaking the paper in vinegar and pressing it to the wound. 'Looks like the ball's gone clean through. Keep this on as a poultice. And sleep with your head to the north. That's about all the doctoring I know.'

He took a look at a Chinese worker who had a head wound, and splashed vinegar on. 'Keep it clean. Don't let the maggots git at it. Sleep with your head high. That's the best way.'

Others of the workers had come creeping back from the hillside rocks where they had hidden, and were clamouring and jabbering, asking for their pay, saying they could not stay. 'Before you get any cash you get spades and help me get a hole dug.'

When they had done so, they slung all the dead into the communal grave and began to cover it up.

'Not Dr Stares,' Miss Luffy said. 'I will send his body back and make an official complaint about his murderer.'

'Lot of good that'll do,' Pete muttered, but hauled his body out of the pit, covering his face with his pith helmet.

He picked up a fallen hat, black, wide-brimmed and low-crowned, with a silver band, and tried it for size. And pulled on a dandy pair of bloodred boots he had taken from a corpse. 'Just my fit.'

'You're not going to rob the dead?' the young woman rapped out in her schoolmarmish manner.

'Waal,' he drawled. 'They ain't no good to him.'

He had also collected the guns and ammunition. 'These might come in handy. It might be an idea if you armed yourself.'

'Me?' Her face expressed horror. 'I couldn't.'

'Please yourself. You don't have to. Only it sometimes helps you stay alive.'

'We had better go,' Judy told him, miserably. 'I've

got the children to feed, the cows to milk, the eggs to collect.'

'Sure, I'll ride along with you.'

'Are you coming back with us?'

'Nope. I'm going into town to give that sheriff a piece of my mind.'

'I'll come with you,' Lucy Luffy said. 'I want words with him, too.'

James Casper was lounging back on a velvet-covered *chaise-longue* in the front upstairs room of the Wild Cat Saloon being shaved by a red-haired young lady, as another, of oriental extraction, knelt beside him and manicured his fingernails. His personal 'maids', or 'masseuses', were a cut up on the two-bit saloon whores. He had imported them specially from St Louis.

'What?' he roared, as the red-head held the cut-throat razor poised. 'Are you telling me that twelve of my men have been gunned down by two men – and they're still alive?'

Bret Spalding stood meekly before him, his Capper & Capper hat in his hands. 'They surprised us. That lousy Injin, and some Texan gun-slinger. We weren't expectin' 'em. You told us just to run off the Chinks and Injun workers.'

'Yes, you nincompoop. And I didn't tell you to shoot down that professor – what's he called – Stares. Nobody's gonna miss a few lousy Chinks and Indians, but there's going to be hell to pay in the eastern Press over this.'

'Aw, Frankie got excited. I'd given him strict orders. Anyway, the Texan cut him down. He's hell fast, that man. And Littlejohn ain't no mean shot with an arrow.'

The oriental girl, slimly sensuous in a snake-tight *cheong-sam* frowned, but carried on with Casper's nails as he leaned back. 'Hold still, honey,' the razor wielding girl cried, and gave a dimpled smile of her rouged cheeks, her piled-up curls like a gleaming auburn helmet.

'Who *is* this Texan?'

'Jedediah Timms, he said his name was. Ain't never heard of him. But he's a professional killer, anyone can see that.'

'Sounds like an alias. We'd better have Hank Lipcott look into him, get a warrant for his arrest. A professional, you say? In that case I'll bring in a couple of professionals of my own. Two can play at that game.'

'We can handle him, Mister Casper.'

'Sure, like you handled him before.'

'There's more than one way of killing a cat. There's no man who can't be shot in the back. And I'm personally gonna take care of that Indian.'

'Careful!' Casper shouted as the girl nicked his cheek, pushing her away, knocking the shaving bowl to the floor. 'Look what you're doing, can't you? Must I be surrounded by idiots?'

The redhead, in her low-fronted, rustling dress, fussed around him, splashing bay rum on his cheeks, fixing his collar to his shirt with studs, tying his tie, tucking it in his waistcoat, fetching the jacket of his suit. 'I'm sorry. You jogged me. Look' – she raised a mirror to his face – 'it's only a nick. Hardly shows.' She dabbed a piece of cotton wool to it.

'Get away.' He waved her off. 'Where can I get a top man? How about Earp?'

'He's retired. Runs a saloon in Denver.'

'What about his sidekick?'

'Doc Holliday? He's in a Colorado sanitarium taking the mountain cure.'

'Who's the best shootist of 'em all?'

'Used to be Hickok, but he got it in the back in Deadwood.'

'What about the Dalton brothers? They operate in these parts, don't they?'

'They got slaughtered robbin' two banks at Coffeyville. Bill Dalton's hiding out in Texas. Didn't you read about it, sir?'

'Cole Younger?'

'In prison. He's got religion, they say.'

'Texas Bob?'

'Got a bad case of respectability.'

'That killer they called Cherokee Bill?'

'Got himself hanged.'

'The Reno brothers?'

'Lynched.'

'How about Clay Allison? He's killed more men than I've had women.'

'Got drunk, fell off his wagon, head crushed.'

'Jeeze, what's the matter with these incompetent fools? Can't they stay alive? I tell you a man who's a true professional, that Cherokee 'breed, Tom Starr. He's robbed more banks than any—'

'Robbed one too many. He's in jail.'

'Hell!' Casper stomped about the room, making the boards shake. 'Send for Doc Holliday. Get him out of his sick bed. Tell him the air's as good here as in Colorado. I'll pay his price.'

'Right, I'll see what I can do.' Spalding pushed a hand through his yellow curls, and headed for the door. 'Hey, I know! That deputy marshal, Frank

Canton. He works out of Guthrie.' Spalding stood
with his hand on the doorknob. 'He did a damn fine
job, him and Tom Horn, putting down nesters in the
Johnson County War up in Wyoming.'

'I don't want a marshal, you numbskull.'

'Marshal, hired killer – same thing as far as
Canton's concerned. He'll kill anyone for five
hundred dollars.'

'Would he kill a young woman?'

'I'm sure he would. His blood's like ice.'

'That Luffy woman. She'll have to be put down.'

'I'll get him, sir. He won't make a mistake.'

Casper glanced at the two girls. 'You haven't heard
this conversation. Savvy?'

The redhead smiled. 'You're talking about the
weather, aren't you?'

And the dark-haired girl shrugged. 'It's lovely out
today, isn't it?'

'Tell him to bring Tom Horn.'

'Can't do that. He got strung up last week.'

'God, let's hope Canton's still alive.'

'He will be. He knows how to survive.'

Casper had moved to the window as the redhead
flicked at his jacket with a clothes brush. 'Talk of the
devil,' he hissed out, 'or devils. They're here.'

Spalding strode over to join him, his duster coat
flapping, his carbine gripped in his big hands. He
peered out of the window and watched as the Texan,
on his quarter-horse, and Lucy Luffy, driving a buggy
with Dr Stares slumped on the back, jogged into
Sulphur Springs down the centre of the dusty main
street, alongside the railroad.

'I can get them now,' Spalding breathed, carefully
poking the carbine through the net curtain of the

open window, and lining up his sights on the Texan's chest. He thumbed the hammer and began to squeeze the trigger.

Casper pushed the carbine aside. 'Have you got spaghetti for brains?' He watched as they passed, their faces grave. They dismounted outside the law office. 'Do you want them fingering me? We're in enough trouble thanks to you killing that professor fellow. Don't do anything off your own bat, you thick-head. I'll do the thinking. We've got to wait and see what card they play. Go on, what are you waiting for? Go tell the engineer to get the Katie stoked up and to head for Guthrie immediately. Tell him to stop for no one. Get Canton. Impress on him the urgency of his mission. Don't you come back without him.'

'No, sir,' Spalding shouted. 'I mean, yes, sir.'

'What we want to know is what you are going to do about it?' the Texan gritted out. 'Are you goin' to let Casper and his thugs get away scot-free? An eminent professor has been killed, apart from several innocent workers. This lady was lucky to escape with her life.'

'I'll investigate.' Hank Lipcott sat behind his desk on his swivel chair, his boots up on a stool, and brushed away a buzzing fly. 'Of course, I will. But, from what you say, if these men were masked, you don't have a lot of proof who was behind it.'

'Who do you think's behind it?' Lucy cried. 'James Casper. Isn't that obvious? Aren't you going to arrest him for murder?'

'If you don't there's gonna be a hell of a stink about this in the Press. You ain't gonna come out smellin' of roses. You gotta decide whose side you're on. That man's gotta be stopped.'

'He's a megalomaniac,' she said. 'He's power-crazed. You've got to arrest him before there are more deaths.'

'Who would that be you are talking about?'

They turned and saw James Casper, neatly turned out in an expensive tweed suit, a gold watch chain across his vest. His handsome features, beneath his brush of hair, bore an amused smile.

'Guess,' Pete snarled.

'They reckon you're behind the killin' of Dr Stares,' Lipcott told him, an exasperated look on his face.

'What? You're joking? That's absurd. I can assure you, Miss Luffy, I saw you bring in his body and I am as upset and astonished as you must be.'

'Like hell,' Pete growled.

Casper ignored him. 'I apologize for our little tiff the other day. My foreman over-reached himself. He thought a couple of slaps might bring you to your senses. My company has been granted the rights to go through that pass. But, as far as foul play or murder is concerned, I am as horrified as you. I would never have condoned such an attack.'

'In that case,' she replied, 'how did you know about it? Who told you?'

'Spalding, of course. He had a mask on but he was easily recognized. He was leading those killers,' the Texan said, jabbing a finger at Casper's chest. 'On your orders. Aren't you going to arrest him, Sheriff?'

'Hold on a minute,' Casper protested. 'If it was Spalding, he certainly didn't act on my orders. He is a fool, a hothead. I admit I have occasionally employed him. But, on this occasion, he must have acted on his own initiative. I would never give such orders.'

'Oh, no,' Pete said. 'Who you tryin' to kid?'

'I assure you, Miss Luffy, I had the greatest regard for Dr Stares. if there is anything I can do? If you are planning to ship his body back East I offer you the services of my railroad free of charge.'

'No, thank you,' she replied, coldly. 'I pay my own bills. You won't get away with this. Don't think you will. I'm sending for a US marshal.'

'I have already sent for one. Don't worry. I'm sure he will investigate this matter with total impartiality. I've asked for Frank Canton. Apparently he's the best.'

'Canton?' Pete muttered. 'Ain't I heard of him?'

'Possibly. I will make Spalding available for questioning. If he is guilty I am sure justice will be done.'

'How about making him available now?'

Casper eyed the tall Texan. 'Unfortunately, he is out of town.'

'He would be. That wounded man of yours told us you were behind this. Did he get back, Sheriff?'

'Yes,' Casper said. 'But, unfortunately, he died from the callous treatment you showed him.'

'He would have, wouldn't he? Are you gonna sit there and listen to this hogwash, Sheriff? Put this bastard behind bars where he belongs 'fore there's more killin'.'

'I can't do that. Mr Casper's a highly respected railroad man. You ain't got a shred of evidence. I gave you my advice yesterday. You better follow it 'fore it's too late.'

'Is that a threat?'

'More a suggestion,' Lipcott muttered, surlily. 'And you, Miss Luffy, might be well advised to accompany that coffin back East. I'd hate to have to send you in your box home, too.'

'You're a disgrace to your badge,' she said, her grey eyes steely. 'Don't think you're going to get rid of me so easily.'

Her dress swished as she left the office, followed by the Texan, and with their exit came the sound of Casper's laughter.

Six

At Windy Ridge, where the gangers had been blasting through solid granite, the locomotive engineer
and his fireman had got the Katie engine steamed up
and headed back towards Sulphur Springs, a jet of
white smoke pumping upwards into the still blue
heavens, the rods pounding rhythmically, the engine
bell clanging mournfully. They had orders from Bret
Spalding to stop for no one, but when they reached
the town they saw James Casper waving them down.
The engineer slammed on the brakes, and the
wheels gripped, sliding along the iron rails in a
shower of sparks. The locomotive came to a standstill
gasping and hissing.

In goggles, his face oily, the driver peered down at
Casper, who shouted, 'Only place you stop between
here and Guthrie is Potototoki Bridge.' He handed
up a slip of paper. 'You pick up these supplies. Only
passenger you wait for is Deputy Marshal Canton.
Then you come on back top speed. OK?'

The engineer nodded and tucked the shopping
list into his boiler suit. He watched Casper go back
past the flatbed goods wagons, one still loaded with a
heavy lifting crane, the passenger car, to the guard's
van.

'Sorry folks,' Casper called to would-be travellers. 'No passengers on this train. You'll have to wait for the weekly Flyer.'

For reasons of his own Casper had halted operations on the railroad that day and the end-of-the-rails town was swarming with graders and tracklayers looking to spend their pay, dedicated Chinese gamblers, hard-drinking Irish navvies. And the grog-sellers, prostitutes and traders, who had flocked to the wide-open town in their wake, were more than ready to service their needs.

The Texan and Jake Hyman, proprietor of a funeral parlour, were pushing through the throng bearing a coffin on their shoulders, accompanied by the slim young woman in her tight-waisted grey dress, and velvet concoction of a hat. As they approached, the guard slid open the side-door of his van and Casper saw Bret Spalding inside. 'Keep out of sight,' he hissed.

In a louder voice the railroad boss shouted out, 'They've got poor Dr Stares in his coffin here. Mr Hyman's got him in a lead-lined casket, or something, so he won't whiff too strong. He's to be transported back East. At Guthrie you transfer him onto the car for St Louis, understand? Here's the relevant documentation.'

He helped Pete and Jake slide the coffin aboard as Miss Luffy watched, and Spalding stepped back into the shadow behind some boxes, his hand on his revolver butt.

'Sure thang, Mister Casper,' the guard said, jumping down, sliding the door to, and preparing to wave his green flag.

Casper drew him to one side and whispered in his

ear, and the guard grinned, blew on his whistle, and hauled himself back up the steps to his van. With a creaking and a clanging and a gasping of steam, the train moved off again, heading out of town. As it did so the burly figure of Bret Spalding, in his long duster coat, emerged onto the back platform. He had his hat in his hand and from beneath that produced a revolver, firing off shots that hissed past the Texan's head, and clanged off a shop sign. Startled, Pete pulled out his S & W and sent a con-catenation of shots in reply. But the train was already out of range, getting up speed, and Spalding stood waving his hat and his revolver, guffawing.

'That half-wit gorilla's beginnin' to git on my nerves,' Black Pete gritted out, and blew down his smoking barrel, in half a mind to go get his horse and set off after them.

'I'm sure it's only Bret's little joke,' Casper smiled. 'He's a tad wild.'

'He's getting away,' Lucy Luffy said. 'You must have known about this.'

'That's alright. He'll be back. He's going on a little errand for me.'

'Yeah?' the Texan muttered, dubiously. 'An' what might that be?'

Casper took his watch from his fob pocket and checked the time, giving them a grin like a Cheshire cat. 'You'll find out, my friend. You'll find out.'

'I've a good mind to plug you now, you mealy-mouthed polecat,' Pete growled, turning his gun on him, 'an' have done with it.'

'You wouldn't shoot an unarmed man?' Casper opened the jacket of his suit to show this was so. 'Not with the sheriff watching?'

Bowen looked across and saw Hank Lipcott standing in his office doorway watching them. 'Yeah, an' that lousy barrel of lard, too.'

'Come on,' Lucy Luffy said, taking hold of his arm. 'Put that gun down. You can't just mow them down.'

'Cain't I? I wouldn't be so sure of that.' He let her draw him away, stepping across the iron rails towards the little telegraph office attached to the railroad booking office. She was about to release his arm but he clapped his fingers over her gloved ones and grinned down. 'That feels good. Like I'm your regular beau.'

'Don't be stupid.' She tried to wriggle her arm free but he was holding her tight. She gave an indignant little snort, but allowed him to escort her through the passing mule wagons and horse riders going to and fro, and up the sidewalk steps to the station. It was, after all, only what any gentleman would do. 'Don't get any funny ideas,' she said, as he relinquished her arm at the door. 'I've had quite enough of men to last me a lifetime, especially those west of the Mississippi.'

She dictated three telegraphs to the man in his green eye-shade, and watched him tap them out – one to Dr Stares' colleagues in New York, one to the US Marshal's office in Guthrie, and one to a senator friend of her father's in Washington.

He took her arm again to guide her across the dusty main drag, more of necessity this time for the traffic was dangerous: three cowboys were whooping and driving a small bunch of frisky longhorns through the moil towards them; a bare-chested Choctaw Indian, feathered and tattooed in fringed buckskins, a blanket around his waist, was riding in the opposite direction on a wild-eyed mustang; and a farmer, with a small child up front of his saddle, was leading a pack mule. Two gents, in top hats and dark city suits, stood outside Cheney's Billiard Parlour, puffing at cigars.

'Doesn't this mixture of peoples typify the West?' Miss Duffy remarked, holding onto her absurd hat.

'I guess it does. The old and the thrusting new.' For seconds he felt the warm swell of her bosom against the back of his hand as he held her back to avoid a covered two-horse buggy. And he experienced a guilty spasm of pleasure at the touch, the scent and closeness of a woman after so long without one, the escape across the desert.

She led him into the bank, the town's only brick building, with ornately false Gothic towers, and he stood back and watched her as she approached the teller's grille. The slender nape of her neck, beneath a wisp of escaped hair where the rest in all its brown luxuriance had been piled up beneath her hat, was very appealing. As also was the jut of her *derrière* beneath the grey skirt, and the sight of her slim-ankled bootees as she bent forward to sign a slip. His dark eyes smouldered and he licked his lips. She had brought him alive. He had an awful longing to kiss that nape, and to kiss on down the whole of her bare, slender body. What wouldn't he give! But the lady wasn't for sale. For all he knew she was still a maid.

Her grey eyes met his as she turned to him, and something in them darkened, like the ripple of water beneath a cloud, questioning him. 'Do you have to stare at me?' she said with a shudder. 'Here.' She thrust a bundle of notes into his hand. 'Five hundred dollars down-payment.'

'Yeah?' He was surprised, because he had only suggested the $1,000 figure thinking it was one she could not possibly pay. But now half the cash was in his hands he was bound to accept. He took one $100 bill and slipped it into his pocket. The rest he took back to the grille, passed them to the teller. 'I'd like this four hundred dollars transferred to a lady's account in Kansas City,' he muttered.

The clerk nodded and took down the details and it was Miss Luffy's turn to watch and wonder. The Texan signed his name with fingers unaccustomed to a pen, and returned to her to pick up his rifle. 'Jest in case I don't live to collect, you could maybe send the rest of what I'm owed to this account.'

'Who's this?' She could not refrain from asking as she glanced at the scrawled name and address on the piece of paper. 'Your wife?'

'No, my first wife's sister. She's looked after my son for ten years. She's seein' him through college now. He ain't gonna be like me. He's gonna be somebody. I only send her what's honest earned. Waal, I mean what ain't stole.'

'Oh?' Her face fell, and she nodded. 'Right. Full payment in that case.'

As they stepped back out into the sunshine he drawled, 'I guess you was worried I might spend it all on whiskey and wild wimmin'?'

'It did cross my mind.' She gave her tight-lipped smile. 'I must place an advertisement in the town newspaper. Casper's scared off all my workers so I need to recruit some more.'

The *Sulphur Springs Star* had been set up in a windowless shack by one of those itinerant would-be journalists who followed the railroads out West.

There were thousands of such rags, most of them short-lived. This one was run by a rat-faced man called Milt Freeman, who had a bad case of dandruff showering his velvet jacket as he sat at his desk in the light of a hurricane lamp and hammered a Remington typewriter. Like most of his ilk he was cynical, drunken, and not averse to bending the truth. He was reporter, editor and printer, and he raked up any bits of scandal he could to turn out on his Washington hand-press. When the railroad moved on and the boomtown died a death he would, no doubt, load up his press, type, imposing stones, ink and paper, and follow it on into the West. For the present he was glad of a circulation of 220 at 25 cents a sheet. He made his money from the advertisements placed by merchants eager to unload their wares on the railroad crews.

'What can I do for you?' he asked.

Lucy Luffy made out her ad. 'Twenty cents a word? That's outrageous. Daylight robbery.'

'Take it or leave it,' he snapped, drily. 'So, you're the bones lady. I hear you been havin' trouble out there. Some kind of war going on?'

'Nothing I can't handle,' she replied, paying him, uninclined to talk.

'Maybe it mighta helped to splash your story,' Pete said, as they left his dark office.

'Perhaps I just didn't like the man. He gave me the creeps. Like something nasty hiding under a stone. Eugh!'

'Waal, I sure have got a thirst. I'm gonna git me a big glass of beer, then I guess we should ride back out to your diggings.' The sun was lowering and his eyes, beneath the brim of his dead man's hat, swept along the skyline of the false-fronted houses, examining every nook and cranny, every open window. He would not put it past young Casper to plant a back-shooter or two. He strolled along the sidewalk past a gunshop, tin shop and mining supplies depot, and paused outside the Wild Cat Saloon. 'You comin' in?'

Miss Duffy relinquished his arm, shaking her head. 'No. I can't enter a place like that. What about my reputation?'

Seven

When the Katie engine reached the pine-pole trestle bridge over the Pototstoki River they slowed down and stopped as instructed. 'What's going on?' asked the driver.

'I dunno,' the fireman said, peering back. 'Looks like they want us to move forward a bit.'

The train jerked forward until it was signalled to stop by the red flag. The guard's van was over the deepest swirling pool of the river.

'That'll do.' Bret Spalding had placed pig-iron inside the coffin of Dr Hyram Stares to weigh it down. He and the guard grunted with the effort as they manhandled it out onto the parapet.

'So long, sucker,' Bret shouted, as he shoved the coffin out and watched it go sailing down to splash into the river and disappear in a cloud of bubbles. 'Nobody's gonna know where he's gotten to. Ain't got a corpse, ain't got a case against me. Or any of us.'

James Casper was discreetly watching Miss Luffy as, the tall Texan by her side, she made her calls about the town. He went into the telegraph office and said to the grey-faced old man in his eye shade, 'What cables did she send?'

'One to New York about Dr Stares' murder and saying his body was due to arrive,' the operator said, handing him it. 'Another here to some senator in Washington. And one to the marshal's office in Guthrie.'

'So she's got the ear of some senator in Washington, has she? "REQUEST IMMEDIATE PRESSURE PUT ON K.T. RAILROAD TO HALT THEIR PROGRESS TOWARDS ARDMORE STOP COMPANY HAS FLOUTED MY WRIT STOP MURDERED MY COLLEAGUE AND WORKERS STOP REFUSES TO RECOGNIZE MAMMOTH SITE AS ONE OF NATIONAL IMPORTANCE STOP" Well *thought* she had his ear.' Casper crumpled the cable and tossed it away.

'She sure says some funny things,' the operator whined.

'Yes, I told you this woman is half-crazed. She'll say anything to protect a few bones. She ought to be in an asylum. You didn't send these?'

'Nope. Just pretended to, tapping my buzzer, but it weren't switched on. Hope you an' the sheriff know what you're doin'. This isn't strictly legal, you know.'

'You've done your citizen's duty.' Casper lit a cheroot and flipped him a double eagle, worth $40. 'That creature will say anything to blacken my name. Calling me a murderer, indeed. I ought to sue. What's this one to the marshal. Blah, blah, blah. "URGENT SEND MARSHAL SOONEST STOP NOT FRANK CANTON FOR PRIVATE REASONS STOP REPEAT NOT DEPUTY MARSHAL CANTON STOP" Huh.' He applied his match to it and let it burn.

'There's another here, sir, for you.'

Casper took it and frowned as he read. It was

from his father, the chairman of the railroad company. 'WHY THE DELAY IN REACHING ARDMORE? STOP DIRECTORS WORRIED STOP QUESTION IN THE SENATE ABOUT SOME MAMMOTH SITE STOP WHAT GOES ON? STOP DO NOT GO DOING ANYTHING FOOLISH AGAIN STOP PROCEED WITH CAUTION STOP REPEAT DO NOTHING UNDERHAND STOP'

Casper tossed that into the waste bin, too. 'The silly old fool never trusts me. He's always breathing down my neck. We haven't got time to pussyfoot around.'

'That so, sir?'

'Yes, it is so. Once this railroad track's a *fait accompli* they'll thank me. We'll be able to start making money. Keep up the good work.'

'Yes, sir.'

When he came out of the office he spotted the Texan outside the Wild Cat Saloon. He appeared to be attempting to persuade the young lady in her wasp-waisted dress and large hat to enter its portals. Casper saw the sheriff watching, too, from outside his office, and gave a flick of his finger to him as he strolled across.

'What's the matter,' he smiled, as he paused beside them. 'Does little Miss Goody Two-Shoes think herself too high and mighty to enter the establishment? Poor fellow, she's really got you under her thumb, hasn't she?'

The Texan bristled at the words and watched Casper push through into the saloon. 'We ain't gonna let him talk to us like that, are we? All I want is to wet my whistle. Then we'll go back to the diggings.'

Miss Luffy drew back, demurely. 'I can't go in that

place of ill repute, especially after what's happened.'

'More reason to. Show the flag. Show 'em we ain't sceered. Just one drink. It's the only saloon in town. Aw, come on, Lucy. Let your hair down.'

'Just one drink,' she said, waggling a finger at his nose.

'Yeah, well, maybe two.' He gently touched the small of her back and pressed her through the swing doors.

Miss Luffy's eyes opened wide as she was hit by a hubbub of noise, saw the throng of men around the gaming tables, others crushed along the bar, heard the screams as two *filles de joie* tried to tear each other's hair out and men roared with laughter, disturbed at their drinking and gambling. A trio of floozies up on a stage were kicking up their yellow-stockinged knees, showing their none-too-clean frills and furbelows, in a rumbustious cancan. Other of their painted sisters were strolling among the men, or hung over those seated, attempting to lure them into the back rooms. Miss Luffy wrinkled her little chiselled nose, half inclined to depart. The lanky Texan caught hold of her elbow and guided her to a table in a corner, depositing his rifle by her side. 'What you havin', ma'am?'

'Oh, I don't know.' She appeared somewhat agitated as raucous Irishmen at an adjoining table leered at her between pouring beer down their throats. 'A lemonade would be nice.'

'Sure. Don't want you gittin' intoxicated or doin' anything you might regret.'

'I don't get intoxicated,' she said primly. 'I like to be in possession of my wits.' She watched him amble to the bar, hips swinging, tall, erect, broad shouldered, his thick, grey-tinged hair hanging over the back knot of his bandanna. He tapped fellows on the shoulder who stepped quickly aside when they saw who he was, avoiding the challenge of his black glittering eyes. 'Gimme a beer an' a lemonade,' he shouted above the din. 'An' a plate of them biled eggs.'

He sank half of the litre of German steam beer in one gasp, telling the 'keep to refill it, before pushing back through to her, balancing the eggs on his glass. The Irish gave him a cheer as he concluded the successful balancing trick. He grinned and slumped down beside her, took another long swig, and wiped the froth from his lips on his sleeve. He peeled an egg, sprinkling salt on it, and took half in one bite. 'Help yourself, Miss Luffy,' he grunted. 'Gotta keep your strength up.'

She did so, if in a more ladylike manner, nibbling at an egg. 'To dispense with formality you can call me Lucy if we're to be thrown together like this.'

'That's a swell name. Sounds lucky. Mine's Pete to you, Jed Timms to others.'

'I hope, however, that you won't go getting any idea that our relationship is any other than a professional one.'

'Sure, I've already received that message, ain't I?' He met her eyes and his face split into a grin. 'Man cain't help but fancy a sweet little body like you, can he?'

'I'm not sweet, nor little, nor do I wish to be fancied. Please understand that.'

'Sure, your body is sacrosanct as far as I'm concerned. I'm an officer an' gentleman, and the epito-mee of a professional. So don't go gittin' any fancy ideas I ain't.'

For some reason she felt a blush rising to her cheeks, and she looked away, busying herself with another egg. 'These are rather tasty.'

'Sure are. And so are they.' He was looking at two girls, two bobbydazzlers, one with gleaming auburn ringlets, the other's black hair fringed and bobbed, both gaudily dressed, descending the stairs on the arms of James Casper, who was wearing his brown Harris tweed suit with a yellow waistcoat. 'Well, I never. What's that canary up to?'

Miss Luffy stared, too, bemused. 'Those beautiful girls,' she said, blinking her eyes. 'Are they—?'

'You got it. Professionals, like me. Sell their services for cash, only in a different way.'

'How dreadful. How degrading for them.'

'Aw, I dunno. Takes all sorts. Gal's gotta make a dollar some how. Mind you, I wouldn't like that monkey pawing me.'

'Nor me,' she agreed, and took a sip of her lemonade. 'Euk! How horrible. Poor girls. Couldn't they do something else?'

'Life ain't so easy if you ain't had an eddy-cation. Or got a rich daddy. Thass why they got a sugar daddy.'

'What's he up to? Why's he stopped work on the railroad?'

'Guess he's playing a cat-and-mouse game.'

She suddenly laughed. 'That's a mixture of metaphors. Canaries, monkeys . . . oh, God, he's seen us. He's coming over here. How I loathe the man.'

'Yeah, what's the slimy sidewinder want now?'

'Surprised to see you in this den of iniquity,' Casper called, cheerily, as he paused before them, a doxy clinging to each arm.

'We're slummin',' Pete growled.

'Aren't you going to try your hand at the tables, Miss Luffy?'

'We stepped in here for some refreshment,' she said, peeling another egg. 'Not to throw money away needlessly.'

'La di da,' the redhead crooned. 'Get her.'

'Please yourself. Might win a fortune. You might need it if you're to hang on to your new boyfriend. He comes expensive, I hear.'

'You hear too much,' she said.

Casper laughed and sauntered away through the press towards the roulette table, the girls squeezing after him.

'The nerve.'

'That fella's asking for trouble.'

'Dat's true, indeed,' one of the Irishmen chimed in. 'I didna' like de way he spoke to de lady.'

'He's your boss man,' Lucy smiled. 'You'd better not pick on him or you'll be out of a job.'

'Maybe that's an idea,' Pete said. 'Organize a mutiny.'

'Well, if he's suspended his blasting operations for a day, perhaps he's having second thoughts.'

'Don't kid yourself, gal. He's waiting for the marshal to arrive to do his dirty work. I don't like the sound of that Canton fellow. He's the one shot down innocent nesters in the Wyoming range war. His side-kick, Tom Horn, just been strung up for killin' a fourteen-year-old boy up there.'

'Yes, I'm glad you told me. I've asked the marshal at Guthrie not to send Canton. Anyone else, but not him.'

'Good for you, Lucy.' Pete watched the puzzled

faces of the grizzled westerners as they saw him
conversing with this respectable-looking lady. 'Maybe
I'll jest git myself a drop of red-eye.'

He got up before she could protest, and at the bar
he saw Casper looking across from the rouge-et-noir
table in a mocking way. To such a hardened drinker
and gambler it was like a challenge. When he got
back he said, 'Guess I'll take a whirl on the tables.'

'Oh, no! You're not going to get drunk and lose all
your money, are you? Drinking and gambling,
they're fools' games. Why do you have to?'

He shrugged and stood up. 'Guess it's too late for
me to change now. Why let the devil have all the fun?
Come on, I'll show you how it's done.'

'You inveigled me in here under false pretences,'
she said. 'All the time you were planning to—'

'Come on.' He grabbed her hands and pulled her
to her feet. 'Time you loosened up, lady.'

'Please let me go. I'll wait outside. How can I possibly, with Dr Stares and those people lying dead? It's
awful. It's indecent. I should be in mourning for
them. What am I doing in here?'

'Aw, the dead are gawn. We're livin'. Hail, gal, you
gotta put on a front. You gotta show these bustards
you don't give a damn about 'em – damn their souls
– whatever they try to do.'

She was flustered as he towered over her, gripping
her hands, the nearness of him. 'You mean,' she
faltered, 'a psychological thing?'

'Don't know about psycho-ogical. Jest show 'em we
ain't gonna be beat.' He put an arm around her and
guided her through. 'He's issued a challenge. Let's
take it.'

'I'm not sure this is a brilliant idea,' she said,

touching a nervous hand to her hat, but letting him keep hold of her other hand. He led her to the roulette table. She forced a smile. 'Mind you, I often wondered just how you played this game.'

'S'easy.' The roulette wheel was presided over by a dark, razor-faced dealer dressed riverboat-style. 'Nuthin' to it. You jest purchase your chips from this gent and place 'em on the number and colour of your choice.'

'Place your bets, boys and gals,' the dealer called, passing Pete chips for twenty dollars. 'All bets on? How about you, lady? Too late, the wheel's spinning.'

They watched the ivory ball go tripping around, until the wheel slowed and stopped and it trickled into the slot awarded by fate. But fate was kind to Pete. He couldn't seem to lose. Whereas Casper and his ladies, on the other side of the table, were on a losing streak and looking decidedly gloomy. Casper topped up the girls' glasses with champagne and scowled across at the Texan who had given a fist-raised rebel whoop. Casper dug into his wallet again.

'I must try,' Miss Luffy cried. 'Can I have two dollars' worth?'

'You surely can.' The dealer gave her a sneering smile. 'Looks like we got the last of the big spenders here.'

This time she gripped Pete's arm as the wheel spun, and pressed her fingers into his biceps excitedly as the wheel slowed. 'Oh, dear, looks like I've lost.' But the Texan was jubilant again as his winnings went up to fifty dollars. 'How *do* you do it?'

'I ain't usually so lucky.'

'Sorry, sir,' the dealer said to Casper as he raked in his chips. 'You lose again.'

'Don't worry, honey.' The redhead, her cheeks powdered and rouged, a false mole by her glistening lips, noted his glum look. 'It's only money.'

'I'll try just once again,' Lucy said, proferring another two dollars.

'Don't git addicted. It ain't worth it.' But Pete's dark eyes were pondering his own chances as he placed chips onto his winning number. 'This sure is something fer me. Normally I'd have lost my hundred dollars by now.'

'Don't talk too soon,' she said. 'Stop while you're winning.'

'Sure, jest one more throw.'

James Casper glowered venomously at them, as he, himself, lost more cash on the red. Pete, too, had lost. But Lucy gave a little cry of delight, as this time she was the winner. She cashed in her chips, delightedly.

'Yeah, reckon it's time to pull out.' The Texan followed suit and pocketed an extra seventy dollars. He leered across at Casper. 'You lose, we win, huh?'

'Not for long,' Casper said, lighting a cigar. He raised his voice and called out, 'Got yourself a new fancy man, have you, Miss Luffy? He wasn't slow to step into the professor's shoes.'

The room fell quiet. For seconds she, too, was shocked into silence by the insulting words. 'I don't know what you are insinuating. I should point out that Dr Stares, who you had killed, was a colleague. This gentleman is my employee. He is not my fancy man, whatever that might be.'

'Your employee?' he smiled, drawing on the cigar. 'Just what kind of employee would that be? How does he charge you – on the length of his poker?'

'I'm paying him to protect me,' Lucy cut in, her voice trembling with embarrassment.

'Really? Well, I doubt if he'll be much good to you soon, either way.'

'Yeah, sweetheart,' the slant-eyed Asian girl purred. 'You better get your money's worth off him while you can.'

The Texan's eyes were like thorns as he glowered at them. 'Don't use that langauge to this lady. You ain't fit to touch the hem of her skirt.' He suddenly gripped the roulette table and pitched it on top of them. Casper and the two girls went down, crashing to the floor amid tumbled furniture, and a clatter of coins, chips and champagne glasses. The railroad boss climbed to one knee, as the girls hung to him, scrambling to right themselves, showing their frilled satin drawers. 'Save it for your whores,' Pete growled, and smashed a clenched fist to the point of his chin.

Casper's head snapped back and his arms flailed as he took several steps backwards and collapsed in a heap.

The Texan pointed a finger at him. 'You better git yourself a gun, mister, 'cause this town ain't big enough for you an' me. I'm ready for you any time. Or you too yeller to try me? You gotta have your boys do your dirty work?'

Casper wiped blood from his lip, but did not reply, lying on the ground as the screams, shouts and commotion died down.

'Hold it right there.' Hank Lipcott had entered the saloon unseen and jabbed a sawn-off into the Texan's back. 'You're under arrest.'

'Shee-it.' The Texan's face looked grim. 'Not

again. I forgot about that damn alarm wire under the bar.'

'What do you mean arrest?' Miss Luffy said. 'Are you mad? Casper here insulted me. Any gentleman would have done what Mr – er – Timms has done.'

'Mr – er – Timms, is it? Mr Bowen more like. Black Pete Bowen, no less. Notorious desperado and murderer. Wanted in Texas for the killing of Old Man Murchison, the cattle baron. OK, boys, we've gotten ourselves a mad dog.' He nodded at two men who had drawn guns. 'Keep him covered. Joe, get that self-cocker outa his jacket. Raise your hands, mister, nice an' easy does it. One false move and I'll blast your spine apart. Jimmy, watch him like a hawk. He's fast.'

The Texan sighed and slowly raised his hands, allowing Joe to take his revolver.

'Good. Now we got the mad dog's teeth drawn he ain't no danger to nobody.' The sheriff gave a howl of laughter. 'Well done, Mr Casper. He fell for the ruse. Get your hands behind your back, Bowen. Hurry, my finger's gitting awful itchy.' As the Texan silently did so, Lipcott snapped iron handcuffs around his wrists, and cackled, 'We got ourselves a real big shootist. There's ree-ward money in this, boys.'

'You stupid fat bastard,' Lucy shrilled, bemused by her own language. 'It's Casper you should arrest. He's a damnable mass murderer. He had six of my workers wiped out, as well as Dr Stares. Are you people just going to stand by and watch this? Mr Bowen's committed no offence in this Territory. Casper's the one who ought to be in jail.'

'Cuff her, boys. She's arrested, too.'

'What? Leave me be,' she screamed, but they roughly got hold of her and, as she struggled, put irons on her wrists. 'I demand to see a lawyer. This is a gross infringement of my rights.'

'Good for you, Sheriff,' Casper drawled, back on his feet, and brushing his suit down. 'What you charging her with?'

'Foul language, insulting an officer of the law, resisting arrest, violation of the city ordinances, frequenting a house of ill fame.'

'You what? All these people are frequenting here, too.'

The sheriff picked up a glass and sniffed it. 'Drinking whiskey, which is forbidden in the Territory, indulging in illegal gambling, and, being a common prostitute, soliciting males for immoral purposes. I reckon she'll draw two years down the line.'

'She sure won't look purty in them striped prison clothes,' some wag laughed.

'You liar,' she screamed. 'You hypocrite. You all are.'

'Stow it, sister. You was seen in the bank passing money to this man who is obviously doin' your pimpin' for you. The game's up.' The sheriff grinned at her and tore the Texan's polka-dot bandanna away. 'See there, that hanging scar. This is him, alright. That's another six months, lady, for harbouring and giving comfort to a wanted criminal.'

'You're insane. You all are.'

'I've telegraphed the Texan Rangers in San Antonio,' the sheriff said, smugly. 'They'll be sending an officer to take this varmint back for his hanging. Everything'll be done by due process of law. He's wanted by the Mexican government, too, for a string of killings. Come on, move.'

'String him up,' a man called, as Pete and the girl were shoved and prodded roughly at gunpoint through the ugly, leering, jeering faces.

'String 'em both up,' a woman croaked, as she tippled whiskey. 'The dirty hussy. Tries to pretend she's so high and mighty.'

'She'll swing high, OK,' another woman yelled, 'if we get in that jail.'

The Texan and the girl were marched over to the jailhouse as the sheriff warned the crowd to keep back. Casper smiled as he watched. 'Perfect,' he said to his girlfriends. 'The law's doing my work for me. They won't get in my way any more. With any luck we might have a little lynching.'

They were locked in separate but adjoining, cage-like cells, still manacled, the barred gates slammed on them.

'Wonderful! Come into the saloon. Let's play a game. What a wonderful idea that was!' the girl called out to him, indignantly. 'A fat lot of good you've turned out to be as my protector.'

'Nag, nag, nag,' he drawled, lying down on the bunk. 'Might have known if I got mixed up with a woman. Never get any peace.'

'I demand to be allowed to contact Washington,' she shrilled.

'Shut up,' the sheriff roared.

'I'd give you your cash back iffen I could,' Pete said, 'but it don't look like I'm goin' to git the chance.'

Eight

James Casper had spent an exhausting evening celebrating his good fortune and, the next morning,
awoke lying between the redhead and the black-
haired girl. 'The scarlet and black,' he liked to call
them. Or '*rouge et noir*'.

He went down into the street in his working
clothes, English jodhpurs and boots, roll-neck jersey
and wide-brimmed hat, and walked over to the news-
sheet shack.

A boy ran out with a bundle of *Stars* shouting its
lurid headline: 'Bogus Bone-Digger Arrested.'

Casper gave him a quarter and studied the story:

The so-called society lady and archaeologist, Miss
Lucy Luffy, 26, was arrested and exposed last night as
a charlatan, extortionist, common prostitute, and
the lover and accomplice of a notorious Texan
desperado.

Luffy posed as a member of the New York
Scientific Archaeology Union and claimed to be
digging up the graves of ancient mammoths, when
all the while she was filling the pockets of her fancy
man.

He was revealed to be Black Pete Bowen, who is

77

wanted in Texas and Mexico for a series of killings, and was arrested at the same time by Sheriff Hank Lipcott in the Wild Cat Saloon. Sheriff Lipcott got the drop on him and the two felons are now lodged in Sulphur Springs Jail.

The sheriff said, 'It is possible, in my opinion, that these two charlatans were responsible for the murder of her unarmed colleague, the elderly Dr Hyram Stares, and the massacre yesterday of several of the Indian and Chinese workers at the site.'

When asked by your *Star* reporter why they should have done this, Sheriff Lipcott said, 'It was a fiendishly clever cover-up so she could tap the funds of the Scientific Union. I believe this frustrated spinster was besotted with the tall Texan killer and, if her claim to come from respectable East-coast society is true, she abandoned her reputation to satisfy her sexual lust and to wallow in sin.'

The Sulphur Springs Saloon has long been under observation as a house of ill fame, where it is believed illegal drinking goes on. In amazing scenes yesterday Miss Luffy was arrested for resorting to the premises for the purposes of prostitution, and was charged with that, unlawful drinking, gambling and unladylike language in a public place.

At the same time the Texan was arrested for physically assaulting a respected businessman, Mr James Casper, junior director of the Kansas and Texas Railroad. Bowen is being held as the killer of Texas cow baron Old Man Murchison. It is understood the Mexican government has also asked for the extradition of Bowen, aged 46, for the attempted kidnapping of their vice president's wife when he murdered 32 of the federal guard.

'She fooled us all,' said Mr Casper, whose company is responsible for bringing prosperity to Sulphur Springs. 'Luffy purported to be unearthing mammoth bones on the path of our railroad. In my opinion they were no more than a few moth-eaten buffalo. She threatened to hold us up at considerable cost unless I secretly paid in thousands of dollars to her account.

'This low and loathesome woman gave the impression of being an upright member of a bluechip East-coast family, a maidenly bluestocking only interested in science, while all the while she was milking the funds of the Scientific Union to give to Bowen to fan his cooling passion. She was, in fact, observed paying $500 to the gunman in the Sulphur Springs Bank, which was then paid into his account. When arrested Luffy had a similar vast amount of cash on her person which testified to her guilt.

'This may sound fantastic,' Mr Casper added, 'but Luffy was so infatuated with the gunman that when Dr Stares, a respected scientist, suspected her devious goings-on, she persuaded the Texan to stage a mock attack on the diggings in which Dr Stares was cold-bloodedly killed, along with other workers. She is such a bare-faced liar she had had the temerity to blame this attack upon me, which, of course, I heartily deny.'

'Fantastic, perhaps, but the truth.' Sheriff Lipcott added. 'I intend to prove this at their forthcoming trial. They are both cold and callous murderers and deserve the ultimate penalty.'

Casper gave a whoop of joy as he went into the gloomy news office and saw the rat-faced Milt

Freeman. 'You certainly know how to rattle out a good story,' he said, taking a wad of $200 from his pocket and slapping it on the desk. 'You've more than earned this. I would say we've cooked their goose.'

The newsman gave him a crooked smile and quickly counted the notes with ink-stained fingers.

When he stepped outside Casper found his foreman, Harry Jones, in his derby and loud check suit, waiting for him.

'Good news, Harry,' he yelled. 'We've cut her legs from under her. It's full speed ahead. We'll carry on with the blasting.'

The two men climbed onto their horses and followed the railroad out towards the gap in Windy Ridge. 'What do you think will happen to those two?' Jones asked.

'The sheriff's going to take a look at the bodies at that scene of the "massacre". There's likely to be several charges of homicide against both of them. They could be tried here. Or the marshal could take 'em back to Fort Smith for their hanging. Or, who knows' – he smirked as he gave the foreman a wink – 'the citizens of Sulphur Springs might take matters into their own hands. Whatever, Harry, we've won the day. Nobody's gonna be stopping us from here on.'

'Here,' Hank Lipcott grinned, shoving a copy of the *Star* through the bars to her. 'Read all about it.'

Lucy Luffy looked at the front page headline – 'Bogus Bone-Digger Arrested' – and the subsidiary headings in heavy capitals – 'Society Woman's Descent into Sin' – 'Accused of Extortion' – 'Her

Lust for Wanted Killer Led Her Astray' – 'They Plundered Scietific Society Funds' – 'Sheriff Uncovers Dastardly Plot' – 'They Murdered Dr Stares to Cover Up' – and the blood drained from her face.

'This is preposterous,' she whispered as she read. Her pale lips trembled. 'How could they?'

Sheriff Lipcott stood, arms akimbo, and shouted, 'Don't like the truth when it's in black and white, do you, you slut?'

'The truth?' She turned to him, her grey eyes staring in their wide whites. 'You call this the truth? Why did you say this?'

'Yeah, Miss Fancypants from New York, thought yourself mighty clever didn't you? Thought you could fool us folks round here. I ain't so dim. I got you figured out.'

Miss Luffy's eyes returned to the newsprint – 'The prisoner was arrested and charged with soliciting for immoral purposes as a common prostitute ... But these are all lies. It's disgusting. The gutter Press. How low can you sink? You haven't given me a chance.'

'You'll get what's coming to you.' The sheriff turned away and gave a wink to his deputy. 'Keep an eye on 'em, Joe.'

'Let's take a look,' Pete said, reaching a hand through the bars for the news-sheet.

They were in adjoining cages of bars in the solid log cabin jailhouse. The sheriff had removed Lucy's manacles, but insisted that the outlaw's remain on. He had, however, allowed him to be cuffed in front of his body so he could eat the lukewarm food on a tin plate shoved under the bars to him.

The Texan squinted at the story and gave a whistle

of awe. 'They certainly got you stitched up, gal. Thass one way of gittin' rid of you. You gotta admire their gall.'

'How can you say that?' she whispered, sitting back on her bunk and looking as if all her life was draining away from her. 'If all these lies get into the Eastern press my life's ruined.'

'Yeah, amazin' how gullible folks are. They'll believe anything they read in these rags. Jest cause it's in black and white they figure it must be the truth. It ain't gonna do a lot for your reputation in high society.'

'I don't give a fig for society. It's my reputation as a scientist that's at stake. Dr Stares and I, we had high hopes these finds would vindicate our theories. To suggest I would . . . it is an utter, foul libel.'

'Yeah, it ain't gonna please my fan club, either. They don't give my side of the story, that's for sure.'

'You–?' She stared at him through the bars. 'You are a killer, aren't you?'

'There, see? They got you believin' it. Sure, I've killed a few I had to. But I don't go round killin' for fun, like they paint me here. If I'd had fair treatment in the first place I wouldn't have gone on the run. But, that's another story.'

'I'm sorry,' she whispered. 'It's just that if I hadn't got mixed up with you they wouldn't have been able to blacken me by association.'

'They would have blackened you either way. That Casper's a neat operator. Here' – he passed the news-sheet back to her – 'and you were right about that lousy skunk of an editor.'

Lucy stared at the news-sheet again, blinking with disbelief. 'What are we going to do?'

'Waal, there sure ain't no way outa here,' he said, going to thump at the solid wall. 'Don't worry, sweetheart, there's no way they can prove that pack of lies against you once you get a lawyer on the job, and a decent marshal to investigate. Not like that lyin' bladder of guts they call a sheriff, over there.'

'By the way,' Lipcott shouted back, 'my deputy Frank's been given the sack. He was caught trying to send a cable to New York on your behalf. So don't go thinking you can smuggle out any more messages. Frank was too soft-hearted.'

'What about a couple of cups of cawfee over here?' the Texan yelled. 'Cain't you see the lady's in a state of shock.'

'What you think this is, a hotel?'

'And another thing,' Pete jabbed a finger through the bars at him. 'We'll need every cent of that cash you took off us accounted for, you thieving cur.'

'Hark to him,' the sheriff laughed. 'Who do they think they are? They won't be needin' it where they're going.'

James Casper called an early halt to the blasting operations that day, and had his foreman pay the workers their coolie wages, plus a bonus. 'Let them know we're breaking open two new barrels of whiskey in the saloon,' he said.

It was only three in the afternoon, so instead of kicking their heels around the campsite, the bulk of the Irish, Chinese, Polish, and other united nations of workers headed for town with their women to mingle with the work-shy riff-raff and deadbeats who had followed the rails west, as well as honest farmers and homesteaders visiting town for market day.

Naturally, the main source of conversation was the notorious killer they had locked up in their town jail, and the scandalous creature, Lucy Luffy, his lover.

The *Sulphur Springs Star* was passed from hand to hand, and those who couldn't read had it read to them. In the town saloon and cathouse the whiskey flowed, and a sense of righteous indignation stirred among the jam-packed crowd as they debated the story.

'That evil Texan has always managed to escape capture,' a barrel-chested German farmer boomed. 'I say we don't give him the chance. I say we should string him up now. The country ain't safe for decent folks with his sort about.'

'I blame that black-hearted bitch as much as him,' an old hagbag who was knitting and drinking at the same time, shrilled. 'There's a mass grave out at that digging site. She deserves the same.'

'Her with all her hoity-toity ways,' another woman shrieked. 'She's worse than him, worse than the lowest of the low. She had that professor killed. I say string 'em both up.'

Most of those in the packed saloon roared their approval, although there were some who looked dubious. 'We oughta leave this to the proper authorities,' a man cried, but his voice was drowned.

Up on the balcony outside his room James Casper watched and smiled. It had cost him a lot of whiskey to get them all fired-up, but it was worth it. 'Nobody crosses me without regretting it,' he said to the redhead. 'I do believe, my dear, we're going to see some fun.'

Over in the jailhouse time had dragged all day. Lucy Luffy had read and re-read the newspaper's vile insinuations with a kind of fascinated horror. She was not sure which rankled most, the suggestion that she had killed her own friend and mentor, Dr Stares, or the words 'frustrated spinster' – the idea that she was obsessed with a killer. Occasionally she met his eyes through the bars. He did not seem such a bad man. In fact, with his unruffled, easy-going manner, he seemed strangely resigned to their dreadful predicament. Or was he? Did he have some secret strength, some hope? Whatever, although she had come to have some sneaking regard for him, it was patently absurd to suggest she was sexually besotted with him. How could she be – with such a man?

As the evening shadows began to fall through the bars of the small window she called out to the sheriff. 'Excuse me. I need to go out back to the privy.'

'Can't do that,' Lipcott shouted. He had slammed and barred the front door. 'It's too risky. You'll have to go in a bucket.' He unlocked the cage and tossed one clattering into her. 'There y'are. Enjoy yourself.'

She stared at the bucket, at the open bars all around. 'How much further am I to be humiliated? This is worse than being an animal in a zoo.'

'What you talkin' about?' Pete asked. 'Too risky? What's going on, Sheriff?'

'You'll find out. Folks gettin' mighty restive out there.'

'It's a lynch mob, that's what it is.' Joe jumped, startled, as stones hurtled through the open window, and they heard raucous shouts outside. 'Hank, maybe we better get 'em outa here?'

The whites of Lucy's eyes flashed in the semi-darkness as she whirled around, looking up at the window, listening, staring with horror, like a trapped animal. There was the thudding of a telegraph pole being used as a battering ram at the front door, cries of men swinging it in unison, the smash of glass as the barred front window was broken. She saw the sweaty faces of the mob in the flicker of tarred flares. 'Bring 'em out!' a man's voice shouted.

'Oh, my God! This can't be happening,' Lucy's dry throat croaked out. 'Tell me this is a nightmare.'

'It's happening right enough,' the Texan said. 'Come on, Sheriff. Hand me my guns. We can hold 'em off.'

Hank Lipcott swallowed his fear. 'You must be joking, mister. You ain't gunnin' any more innocent people down.'

'You call them innocent?'

The door was creaking under the pounding, and the shouts outside had increased in intensity, like the sound of hounds baying for blood. The noise had become like a roaring in Lucy's ears, and she clapped her hands to her head, sank to her knees, as if to blot it all out.

'OK,' Pete shouted, 'Throw me to 'em. I'm ready to go. But don't give 'em her. She's nothing to do with this. Come on, Lipcott. Be a man for once in your life.'

It was too late. The door burst open. The leaders of the mob surged in, two of them brandishing ropes in their hands. Hank Lipcott and Joe backed away, their carbines held across their chests. 'Get out of the way, Sheriff,' a man shouted, wildly. 'You ain't stopping us.'

'Take the man, boys. But not the girl,' Lipcott stuttered out. 'Maybe it ain't true. Maybe she's innocent. She deserves a trial. Don't do this, boys.'

The wild-eyed mob was like a monster of one mind. By sheer numbers they thrust the sheriff and his deputy aside, snatched the keys, unlocked the cells and dragged the Texan and Miss Luffy out.

'She is innocent, you damn fools!' Pete shouted. 'I ain't, but she is. Leave her be.' He could say no more, his head jerked back as a noose was tightened around his throat.

There was a roar of drunken approval from lusty throats as the two of them were led from the jail. Ruddy faces under flickering torches stared at them, hungrily. 'Make the whore kick air,' a woman shrieked. 'She's a shame upon her sex.'

'Yes,' came a shout of approval as a hempen noose was fixed around the archaeologist's neck. 'Let 'em swing together.'

Willing arms dragged them across the main street to an open wagon, its two horses standing idle. The man and the girl were hoisted bodily on to it. 'Tie her hands,' a man shouted, as he sent the rope around her neck spinning up over the arm of a telegraph pole. He fixed its end almost tight, so her toes had to take the strain. Pete glanced at her as they did the same to the rope around his throat. He held himself, contemptuous of the gloating faces beneath him. It was a fate he had been expecting a long time. He experienced a sense of sorrow only that she had to go, too.

'Any last words?' a man demanded.

'Boys, you're making a big mistake,' he croaked out – 'about *her*. Cut her free.'

Lucy stared at them defiantly, as they spoke to her. 'Go to hell,' she said. 'All of you. I refuse to be judged by you.'

The women laughed, the men jumped clear, and the horses were about to be whipped forward when an arrow hissed through the air, neatly severing the rope above the girl's head. Another arrow half severed the rope over the Texan's hair. At the same time there was a flash and the roar of an explosion of dynamite on a fuse beneath the sidewalk behind them. The crowd scrambled away in panic. The wagon horses started forward, jerking the Texan back. The impact broke the last strand of rope. The girl tumbled down on top of him, hanging on to him as the wagon went bouncing away down the road.

'What the devil?' Pete muttered, as her cheek brushed his, her hair in his face. 'Am I in heaven or what?'

There was a rattle of galloping hooves. Pete looked back and saw Howling Wolf charging through the scattered mob, hanging low over his spotted grey stallion, drawing alongside them, the quarter-horse on a trailing rope, whinnying as she was dragged along. The Wichita grinned across at them, galloped on and caught hold of the wagon horses, slowing them as they cleared the outskirts of the town. He returned, and slashed free her hands.

'Howdy, partner,' he called. 'You didn't think I'd let them hang you, did you?'

'You took your time,' Pete said. 'That was a close call.'

He leapt from the wagon onto the back of the quarter-horse. 'Come on,' he called to Lucy. 'Jump on behind me. What you waitin' for?'

The young woman glanced back at the mob, some of whom were surging towards them, howling their anger and disappointment, the blazing tar brands in their hands. She quickly hoisted her skirts and slung a pantaletted leg over the back of the horse. She gripped him around the waist and pressed her face into his broad back as they went surging away, bullets whipping through the air about their heads. She suddenly began to sob, whether it was with relief, surprise, joy, or shock, she did not know. She knew only a great sense of elation as she hung on to the Texan and they went galloping away through the night.

Nine

Howling Wolf led them through rocky chasms until they reached the dark outline of a cave entrance in a granite wall. He jumped down and cried, 'Welcome to my hideout.'

Lucy slipped from the quarter-horse and asked to be excused. She scrambled away behind a rock. She had been longing to go since being in the jailhouse. What blissful relief. She had feared the further humiliation of wetting herself before those horrible people. They would have seen it as a sign of cowardice. And. even though nothing should have mattered to her when so close to her death, she was determined above all not to be seen as a coward. She straightened her skirt and watched the cold globe of moon begin to rise above the harsh, interweaving ranges of the Arbuckle Mountains, painted silver by its glow. She shuddered at the memory of what had happened.

The two men were shaking hands and chuckling together when she returned. 'It's like the old days, eh, Pete?' Henry grinned. 'I ain't had no action like this for years.'

'You OK?' the Texan asked her, and she nodded,

gave her tight-lipped smile in reply. 'Good gal,' he said, giving her a grin.

'So, what are we going to do now?'

'I came prepared,' the Wichita said, unrolling blankets from the back of his saddle and tossing one to each of them. 'I got hammer and chisel so first we get Pete's manacles off.'

The Texan sighed and rubbed his wrists as the irons fell free. 'Thank God for that.'

'I got some grub. We can make a small fire inside the cave. They won't find us tonight.'

They led their horses into the spacious cave, and soon had a fire flickering. Henry crushed coffee beans under the butt of his Dragoon revolver and boiled up water in a battered enamel pot. He carved slices of bread and roast wild turkey and passed them across.

'What I meant was,' she said, as she sat with her back to the rock and sipped at the steaming coffee, 'What are we going to do tomorrow?'

Pete scraped fingers through his thick hair and his dark eyes glowered at the memory of the rope around his neck. It was the third time he had cheated such a death, and it always gave him a strange sense of being in some other world, suspended between the real one and that of the shadows.

'They'll come after us,' he said, 'But they ain't gonna git us. I got guns and ammo stashed back at your diggings. We'll take a stand. We ain't gonna let Casper and his damned railroad through.'

'Really?' She sounded startled. 'Is that a good idea? I really think it might be wiser if I tried to reach Fort Arbuckle and civilization, sought some justice. And you – well, you should go on to wherever you were going. This isn't a game we're playing. That's twice they've tried to kill us.'

'I bet you didn't like the feel of a hempen necktie, Miss Luffy? Your first time? Pete, he's got used to it.'

'Hopefully the last time. No, I certainly didn't. I've really had enough. They'll send a posse after us now. What can we do against such overwhelming odds?'

'I dunno,' Pete muttered, as Howling tossed him his tobacco pouch and he rolled himself a cigarette. 'But I hate to let them varmints run us off.'

She sat silently for a while, watching the fire slopping weird shadows across the cave walls. 'How did I get into this?' she sighed. 'OK, I'll stay.'

'Good gal.' The Texan rolled up in his blanket and stretched out beside the fire. He patted the ground beside him. 'Why don't you git some sleep over here? It's alright, nobody ain't gonna hurt you.' He grinned across at Howling Wolf. 'Only I don't trust that Injin. He's a horny bastard. I've had trouble with him before.'

Henry smiled at Miss Luffy. 'It's that *hombre* you don't wanna trust. You're safer where you are.'

She twisted her lips, quizzically, and smiled, picking up her blanket and going to lie down beside the Texan. 'Guess I've got to trust him. Anyway, I've paid him enough. And am I not supposed to be his fancy lady?'

Pete grunted, and tipped his hat over his eyes. 'Some hope of that.'

'By the way, Henry,' she called, as she rolled herself in her blanket. 'Thank you for rescuing us. I do hope you haven't put your family at risk. You must take them somewhere safe away from here.'

'Nowhere's safe,' he muttered, 'where white man is.'

In the night Pete awoke. There was a slim arm
lying across his chest. In the light of flickering fire
embers he saw that she had snuggled into him. When
he moved her hand tightened and she pressed her
soft cheek against his bearded jaw. 'I wanted to thank
you, too,' she whispered, 'for seeing me through this.
But I didn't know how to.'

He leaned on one elbow and tossed another log
on the fire. He reached across and smoothed her
hair from her brow, his eyes glowing in the flamelight
as they met hers, and he gently cupped her cheek
with his long fingers. 'Go to sleep,' he said.

'I'm not sleepy.'

Her cheeks were flushed by the fire, her thin,
intelligent face intent as she studied him, her grey
eyes, with their clear-outlined aureolas, uncertain,
but questing. He gently tested her lips. They were
firm and unresponsive . . . at first. But, gradually, she
responded to him, reaching fingers up to scrape
through his hair, and her lips opened to him, as he
slipped his tongue into the mouth's cavity, warm and
moist. He dibbled his tongue against her's and whispered, 'What about Henry?'

'He's sleeping,' she murmured.

He glanced across and checked that it was true.
The Wichita was lying on his side, his back to them,
breathing heavily. He turned back to her, and began
undoing the front buttons of her dress. She lay staring at him, wildly, as if before a crisis, her bosom
heaving. He prised her breasts from her bodice and
dipped his head to kiss and nibble at their pink,
uptilted tips.

'Please be gentle with me,' she begged.

'We'll just take it nice and easy,' he muttered,

drawing up her skirt and petticoats.

'They all think I'm a loose woman,' she moaned, defiantly, opening her arms to embrace him,. 'So, why shouldn't I be?'

Howling Wolf was awoken by the rustle of clothing, a whispering sound. He reached out, automatically for his scalping knife, and saw the giant shadow thrown by the fire onto the cave roof above him – a long-haired demon rearing rythmically over a girl. 'The wicked old goat,' he muttered, grinning to himself. 'He sure don't waste his time.

Judy was awoken in the darkness before dawn by the thud of hooves outside their cabin, men's guttural shouts, the rattle of gunfire. As the windows smashed and bullets thudded into the walls, she screamed and rolled out of bed with the baby in her arms. 'Get down!' she cried, snatching at Bess's thin arm, pulling her from her cot on top of her, and huddled trying to protect them as explosions of firearms thundered from all around the cabin, and lead whistled and crashed into furniture and crockery, cutting it to smithereens.

'We got you surrounded,' a man shouted. 'Come out with your hands up.'

'Stay put,' she whispered to the children. 'Don't move.' In her white nightdress she clambered to her feet and went to peer out of the bullet-riddled door. 'There's only me in here,' she screamed, 'an' my kids. Don't shoot!'

'Bring 'em out,' the man roared at her. 'And don't try any fancy tricks.'

Judy padded on bare feet through the broken

glass to collect the whimpering little girl, and her baby brother, who was howling lustily by now. 'We're coming out,' she yelled, and carefully stepped out with them onto the veranda, half expecting to be decimated by bullets.

Sheriff Hank Lipcott showed himself, rising up from one knee with his shotgun at the ready. 'Where is he?' he hollered. 'If he tries anything you get it first. You hear that Howling Wolf?'

'He's not here,' Judy pleaded. 'Please, don't shoot no more.'

Lipcott strode warily towards her as other men showed themselves from behind the barn and the corral posts, stepping out into the moonlight, carbines raised. Lipcott beckoned her out into the yard, jumped onto the veranda, kicked in the shattered door, and blasted another volley into the cabin. 'Come out, you varmint.' His second barrel flashed scatter-lead into the bed, making feathers fly. And he stepped back out, reloading the twelve-gauge.

'She's right. The bird's flown.'

'What do you want with him? What's he done?'

'Don't tell us you don't know.' His deputy, Joe, stuck his dark-jawed face close to hers and grabbed her by the neck of the nightdress. 'You Injin-lovin' bitch, where's he hidin'?'

Judy's hair was as pale as her frightened face in the moonlight. 'I don't know where he is. He hasn't been home since yesterday evening.'

Joe shook her, making her teeth rattle and the children scream more. 'Leave me be,' Judy cried, gasping for breath as he half throttled her, hanging on to the children. 'Why are you doing this?'

'He's only snatched that damn Johnny Reb outlaw

friend of yours, and his ladyfriend, from under our noses and the hands of a lynch mob, thassall,' Joe shouted into her face. 'If it weren't for these brats we'd make you talk, sister. Cain't you stop 'em cater-wauling?'

'Leave her be, Joe,' the sheriff said. 'They ain't here. Come on, boys, we're wasting ammunition and time.'

The bulky Lipcott hauled himself onto a mustang and pointed a finger at her. 'Your husband's a wanted man. There's no way he can evade justice. He's as good as dead.'

Judy stood staring after them, trying to console the children, as the men rode away into the darkness. 'Jeez,' she whispered, 'Henry's sure got hisself into a passel of trouble now.' She went back into the cabin and surveyed the wreckage. 'Those men don't mess about, do they?'

Lucy Luffy buttoned her blouse to the throat, and tried to tidy with her fingers the hair that had fallen wildly about her shoulders. 'What time is it?'

'Time we were gittin' goin'.'

'I rather like being a loose woman,' she smiled.

'At least they cain't call you a frustrated spinster no more.' He grinned, as he sat up and rolled a ciga-rette.

'No, they certainly can't.'

'I got the impression I weren't the first, which was a kinda surprise.' He put the coffee pot on the embers to boil. 'But, then, ain't much surprises me no more.'

'Is it so surprising that a young woman might have had an affair?' she asked. 'Oh, it was a long time ago.

I was really just a girl. He swept me off my feet, had his way with me. I was truly besotted with him.'

'So, what happened?'

'He was what they call a cad, a bounder. He made a practice of deceiving naive girls.'

'He left you in the lurch ... standing at the church?'

'Not exactly,' she smiled. 'But almost. Fortunately, I saw through him. It was I left him.'

'Since when –' the Texan handed her a mug of the steaming tarry liquid – 'you've dedicated yourself to studying the long dead?'

'Exactly.' She winced as she took a sip. 'I decided a good while ago that living men are extraneous to my needs.'

'More trouble than they're worth, the nasty, smelly things.'

'Exacty. You said it, buster.' She stared into the coffee deep in thought. 'You're my second man, believe it or not. I really don't know what came over me.'

'Doncha?'

She gave him a brief smile. 'Don't think it signifies anything. I'm not planning on being your floozie.'

'You don't fancy riding along with a wanted outlaw? No, I can see your point there.'

'It was just a spur of the moment thing,' she said, indignantly. 'My way of saying thank you. It won't happen again.'

'A very nice thank you.' He got to his feet. 'Hope you figure I was worth a thousand dollars.'

'Every cent,' she called, as he left the cave, and murmured to herself, 'I had really forgotten what I was missing.'

*

'Soon as she opens her mouth something sharp comes out,' he muttered, as he climbed down to a stream to wash. 'We were content up to then. But I guess she don't want me to get no romantic notions. Independent little body.'

A red rim of flickering fire illumined the eastern horizon preluding the dawn. Pete stared out across the mountainous ravines stretching away, etched against the ruddy sky. 'Not a soul in sight. Trust Henry to find a nice li'l hidey-hole,' he said. 'How the hell did I git mixed up in this?'

He collected kindling and, with the bundle of brushwood under his arm, returned to the cave.

'Wake up, Hiawatha.' He dug Henry with his boot and handed him a mug of coffee. 'Sun's rising and it sure feels good to be alive.'

'I bet it does,' the Indian remarked. 'You been celebrating that fact, eh? Both of you?'

Miss Luffy's cheeks reddened. 'Is there anywhere I can wash,' she quickly asked.

'All mod cons,' Pete said. 'Just down the hill.'

When she had gone, Howling Wolf grinned at him. 'You smelly ole polecat. Who'd'a thought that fine educated lady—'

'When they're icy on top there's usually a volcano smouldering below,' the Texan said. 'I feel kinda strange not havin' a gun, or even a knife. That sheriff's got my hundred dollar Creedmore, an' my S & W, not to mention my cash. We better push on to the diggings. I ain't gonna be much good like this in a fight.'

'I could always make you a bow, Black Pit.'

'Yeah.' He went to fondle the liver-and-cream quarter-horse, which he had kept loose-saddled in case of emergency. He jerked tight the double cinch, and investigated the saddle-bags. Yes, it was still there, buried beneath some musty socks, the new-fangled Mauser the American tourist had surrendered to him down in Mexico. It was small and compact, T-shaped, bullets fed in through the grip. Only .32 calibre. 'What they call a pocket plinker,' he said, showing it to Henry. 'But better than nuthin'. There's two slugs left in.'

'That's two less of the enemy.'

'Not with this thang, it ain't. Thanks for rescuing my hoss, by the way.'

'I'm worried about Judy and the kids,' Henry said, tossing back his shoulder-length black hair and tying his headband tight. He squatted by the fire and whirled the cylinder of his converted Dragoon. 'Something tells me they're in trouble.'

'I don't think any white man's going to hurt a woman and children,' Pete growled, lighting a ciga-rette with a burning twig.

'Oh, no? Who you kidding? What about Custer when he killed women and children, wiped out my people's peaceful camp on the Washita?'

'They were Injins and we were in a state of war – not that I'm excusing that. But Judy's white. Best thing is you better stay away a while.'

The Indian sipped at the mug of scalding coffee. 'What's your plan of campaign, lootenant?'

'I ain't got one,' Pete grinned. 'But when I led the First Cherokee Cavalry down here I allus believed in taking the war to the enemy.'

'Sounds a good idea to me,' Howling Wolf said,

tossing the coffee dregs aside. 'I go prepare myself.'

Lucy Luffy returned, looking refreshed. 'I wish I had a comb.' She smiled, apologetically, as she tried to pin her hair up. 'I feel a bit of a wreck. A tooth-brush would help, too.'

'Aw, quit fussin',' he said, handing her a slice of cold turkey. 'You look fine to me.'

'Well, I expect you're used to living out in the wilds.' She looked up, startled, as an eerie moaning sound keened through the cave behind them. 'What's that noise?'

For some moments he, too, was puzzled, then he grinned. 'There must be a kinda chimbley-hole up through the cave. Thought as much the way the smoke drifted away. That's ole Howlin' prayin' an' chantin', preparing his soul for battle.'

'He' – she looked uneasy – 'he really believes in that?'

'Sure does. They sent him off as a kid to a college in the East after the war. Some do-gooders arranged it under the Reconstruction Plan. Thought it would benefit the Indian, help 'em hang onto their rights. Some hope of that. All it did was fill Henry's head with a lot of useless knowledge about Plato and the ancient Greeks. Now he's trying to get back in touch with his ancestors. Jest listen to him moo-ha-hahing up there!'

'So you don't believe in accumulating knowledge?' she asked, sharply. 'Or even in the Indian's religious powers?'

'I believe in knowing thangs that might be some use keeping a man alive out here in the wilds. He'd have been better off learnin' how to build a birch bark canoe and suchlike. What I'm sayin' is Henry's got a split-personality. He ain't sure what he is.'

'So you make mock of both sides? His acquired European culture and his – chanting?'

'Nope. He kin chant all he likes far as I care. I don't underestimate the Indian mentality. They know things we've only an inkling of. You wouldn't believe the things I've seen. The Moqui dancers, live rattlers in their teeth . . . aw, I could go on all day. But, in the long run, all their magic didn't do 'em much good, did it, against the whites' military might?'

'No, I suppose not. But that's not reason to mock their culture.'

'Gosh, you're a feisty gal, aincha? First thing in the mornin', allus ready for an argument. Git that grub down ya. We gotta move.'

'Where are we going?'

'Lady,' he said, standing up, 'we're going to make war on them dogs in Sulphur Springs. First we gotta go back to your camp, arm ourselves, prepare. Then we get ready to hit.'

'My first priority is to protect those finds we've already got packed up. I had planned to send them east on the railroad, but that's no longer possible.'

'No, that ain't a feasibility. Doncha worry, we'll think of something. Thass what this whole war's about, ain't it, far as we're concerned, protecting them mammoth tusks?'

Lucy smiled and stood up, brushing herself down. 'Good.' She touched his waist and paused as she passed. 'I'm glad you know what we're fighting for. It's not just vengeance?'

'Lady,' he grinned. 'I been fightin' for lost causes all my life.'

'This isn't a lost cause.' The black pupils of her grey eyes widened as they locked with his. 'At least, not as far as I'm concerned. And don't call me lady. Why are you suddenly so aloof?'

'I ain't aloof. I'm jest worried. We got a fight on our hands.'

Ten

'Wah! Wah! Wah!' went the steam whistle as the Katie engine rattled back along the rails into Sulphur Springs. The front bell clanged as the engineer eased her into the station, and the locomotive stood gasping and wheezing after the long haul from Guthrie. A tall, thin man, in a round-bowled, wide-brimmed black hat stepped out onto the running board and looked around him before stepping down. He had a rifle in one hand and, like his companion, Bret Spalding, wore a long duster coat over spruce clothes. But, unlike the bouncer, who bustled about, the tall man's actions were tense and coolly deliberate. He gave the impression of a rattler coiled and ready to strike.

'We'll go over to the saloon,' Spalding said. 'See if Mister Casper's there.'

'We better had,' Frank Canton replied. 'I don't work 'less I get cash up front.'

For his thirty-or-so years he was babyfaced, or boyish, clean shaven except for a thin Mongolian moustache which drooped around his mouth, grown, perhaps, to give him a look of greater authority. As they entered the Wild Cat's shady, seedy interior he gave a down-turned grimace, glancing at the scruffy men gathered about the gaming tables, at the prairie nymphs in their frills and fol-de-rols, their gartered stockings, sprawled along one wall.

'Presumably this is the joint you preside over?'

'Yeah,' Spalding mumbled. 'Mister Casper took over the top floor when his railroad hit town. For his headquarters, like.'

'Really? I would have thought he could find more salubrious accommodation.'

The bouncer shrugged and led the way upstairs. He had got used on the journey down to the dude's fancy way of talking. He didn't much strike him as a fast gun, but, then, appearances could be deceptive. He hadn't thought much of the Texan when he first arrived. 'The boss in?' he asked a gunman who was leaning over the balcony rail.

'Sure.' The bodyguard faced up to Canton. 'I need to take your guns, mister.'

'Nobody takes my guns offen me.' Canton eyed him with a straight, steely look. 'Unless I'm dead.'

'Thass OK, Abe. This is the famous marshal, Frank Canton,' Spalding chuckled. 'Or infamous.'

'And, you,' Canton turned at the door and jabbed his rifle into the bouncer's gut. 'You keep making those funny remarks you won't be with us long.'

'Sure, sure, Frank, just bein' friendly,' Spalding said, knocking, and ushering him in. 'This here's the boss, Mr Casper. Well, here he is, Boss.'

'Welcome,' Casper said, getting up from studying some drawings on his desk, and offering his hand. 'So you're the big man I been hearing about?'

Canton ignored his hand, tossed his Gladstone bag down, and looked around at the spacious room. At one end, on a big mahogany bed, two finely

dressed girls were sat billing and cooing like a couple
of doves preening themselves, peering into a hand
mirror.

'The one with the auburn ringlets is Rosie, my
masseuse. That li'l Eurasian beauty calls herself My
Ling. She's my secretary.'

'Get rid of 'em.'

'Oh, right. Just who's giving the orders round
here?' Casper snapped his fingers. 'Girls, wait down-
stairs.'

When they had gone Canton removed his gloves
and his wind-shedder coat, and stood immaculate in
a pair of tight grey peg-top trousers, silver-enscrolled
boots, a cross-over vest of watered silk, and a black
frock coat cut away for easy access to the stag-horn
handle of the revolver that jutted from the holster
tied to his thigh. A US deputy marshal's badge was
pinned to his waistcoat.

'What can I get you? Brandy?'

'I'm a temperance man. I like to keep a cool
head.'

'Well, maybe a glass of sarsaparilla. Bret, see to it.'

'So, what's your price?' James Casper asked when
they were alone. 'I understand you people don't
come cheap.'

'What for?'

'Killing a man and a young woman. I've been kicking and cursing myself. We had them in our hands,
but some lousy Indian rescued them. Uses a bow and
arrow, would you believe?'

For the first time an icy smile spread across
Canton's mouth. 'An Injin? Sounds like I'm getting
mixed up with a right collection of idiots.'

'We all make mistakes.'

'So that's three you need putting down. The man, he's some kinda shootist?'

'Black Pete Bowen. There's reward on his head in Texas.'

'Yeah, I heard of him. The girl?'

'Comes from some society family back East. Miss Lucy Luffy.'

'Hmm?' Canton rubbed his chin as he considered this. 'That puts my price up. There's bound to be questions. Can't do this job for less than five hundred dollars each, them two. The Injin's nuthin'. Say two hundred and fifty dollar shares in your rail-road. Paid in advance.'

'In advance. But how do I know—?'

'You want the best, don't you? Everything will be done so it appears legal. The girl will get in the way of a bullet. Unfortunate, but these things happen to the best law officer. Or am I wasting my time?'

'No-o. That sounds fine. The sooner you get it done the better. We're behind schedule. I got the directors breathing down my neck.'

'These maps of the railroad?' Canton asked, going to the desk.

'Yes.' Casper pointed a finger. 'We've got to here. We've blasted through Windy Ridge. We can wind up through the Arbuckle Mountains for about ten miles, but then we reach this ravine. That's where this woman, Luffy, has her camp. She's digging up mammoth bones and suchlike. She reckons that land's sacrosanct and she's got a writ preventing us going through. I plan to ignore that. With her silenced there'll be no more opposition.'

'Can't you go any other route?'

'No, impossible. My surveyors say it's the only way.

She's blocking our direct progress south to Ardmore and the Red River. This line is most important. It means that, instead of being herded, cattle from Texas can be shipped by rail all the way up to Kansas to join the main railroad east. That stupid young woman's standing in the way of progress.'

'That's probably not how she sees it.'

'Read this.' Casper handed him the *Star*. 'Bone-Digger Arrested.'

Canton studied it and smiled again. 'You mean you had 'em both safely tucked up in jail? What the hell you let 'em go for?'

'Some damn necktie party got 'em out.' James Casper couldn't help reddening up as he remembered how his plan had gone awry. 'Then they got away.'

'Heck!' Canton gave a gasp of mocking laughter. 'You people! You need your heads lookin' at. Run a railroad? You couldn't run a damn nursery.'

There was a knock and Spalding stumbled in with a glass of sarsaparilla, which half spilled onto the tray from the glass.

Canton took it and tossed it over Spalding's shirt front. 'You might as well have the rest.'

'Right,' James Casper said. 'if you'll accompany me over to the bank, Mr Canton.'

'I'll be needing a decent horse. Provided by you, of course.'

'See to it, Bret. We've got no time to lose.'

When they reached the diggings site Miss Luffy was relieved to find most of the expedition's tents and belongings still intact. 'What a relief to be able to change my clothes,' she cried.

'We ain't got time to hang about,' the Texan said, going to examine the stash of captured revolvers and carbines, picking himself out a couple of sturdy items, and spare ammunition belts.

'You're not abandoning the site? I thought we were going to protect it.'

'It's too exposed. We can protect it better by not being here.'

'But what about my tusks? The other finds? I wouldn't put it past those fiends to smash them up in an act of petty revenge.'

'We sure cain't carry 'em with us. Best, maybe, to hide 'em.' He went over to a makeshift corral, caught hold of a couple of the mustangs once belonging to Casper's gunmen. He tied lariats around the two packing cases, and looped the ropes around the mustangs' necks. 'We'll drag 'em over to that stand of pines, hide 'em. They ain't likely to look there.'

'Please be careful. Those artefacts are very precious.'

'Aw, it's flat, sandy ground. They won't get hurt.'

When he and Henry got back Miss Luffy was busy cooking up a lunch of pancakes for them, and had opened a can of lobster.

'No, I can't eat that,' the Wichita said, horrified. 'That's the devil fish.'

'Don't be silly. It's scrumptious. I thought you were an educated man?'

'Who's mocking his sincere beliefs now? That fish is bad medicine. Don't you eat it, Henry. Pass it over. I'll have your share.'

After lunch, Lucy went to search through her piles of books and sheafs of notes.

'We ain't got time for that,' Pete shouted. 'We gotta travel light. We'll just carry rations for a coupla days – flour, dried jerky, coffee beans. Bullets is what we need most. You'll ride that mustang. So, before you start changing your clothes, here.' He tossed her a pair of denim jeans. 'Put these on, an' these long johns. They keep you warm and stop the stirrups chafing your legs.' He dug into some clothes he had taken from the gunmen's bodies after the fight. 'Here's a shirt and leather jacket should fit you. Here's a decent pair of boots. And find yourself a hat and slicker. Weather's fit to break.'

'Dead man's clothes,' she muttered, disgustedly, as she went behind some boxes to tog herself out.

'Yeah. And maybe a disguise. They'll be lookin' for you. It's obvious they want you dead, same as me.'

'Dead?'

'Yeah, as a dodo. Ain't that dawned on you yet? What do you think that lynching was all about? They don't want you to bother 'em any more.'

'I just can't believe it.' She wriggled into the denims. 'That, anybody would stoop that, that low.' She puffed as she pulled the boots on. 'Just to get a railroad through here.'

'You better believe it. You better be ready to ride fast. And to shoot to kill.'

'Shoot?' she jammed a Stetson over her pinned up hair. 'I can't shoot. I can't kill.'

'Kill or be killed,' he said. 'It's that simple.' She stepped out from behind the boxes and he gave a whistle. 'Wow! Behold, a handsome young cowboy. Come on, I'm gonna give you a lesson.'

'A lesson?'

'A shootin' lesson.' He went outside, placed some empty bottles on a rock, stuck a Colt .45 in her hand. 'Try your luck.'

'What do I do?'

'Cock it, aim it, fire. It's simple. They're only twenty paces off. You can't miss.'

The young woman bit her lip, raised the Colt, which wavered in her grip, trying to squint along the sights, pulled the trigger and fired. The revolver kicked as it reverberated. She let loose all six, determinedly, and stood swaying in a swirl of blue powder smoke, listening to the echoes of the shots bouncing off the ravine walls.

'Or maybe you can.' All the bottles were still standing. 'Look. It's easy.' He took the Colt from her and fanned the hammer in one single stream of explosions. When the smoke cleared only one of the bottles was still standing. 'Yeah, well, it ain't really my kinda gun. Prefer double action.'

He took the Mauser from his back pocket and drawled. 'This popgun might be better suited to you. Ain't so heavy. Ain't got much of a kick.' He stood behind her, his arms around her, and showed her how to grip, how to be ready for the recoil. 'You goin' for a heart-shot aim for the belt buckle,' he growled in her ear. 'You gotta think "Kill". Don't hesitate. Or you might be too late. Take your aim just below that first bottle. Now, a gentle pressure. Go! That's better. Again! You got it. Again! Oh, no. There ain't no more in. I'd better try find some .32 calibre.' He had his body jammed into her spongy buttocks, and pulled her tight, breathing into her ear. 'You'll make a shootist, yet. You only need practice.'

'Please,' she shuddered. 'Don't.' She wriggled out of his clutches. 'You make me feel funny. I – I just couldn't kill anyone. Perhaps I will aim at a leg, or arm.'

'No you gotta go for a body shot. Don't worry, gal.
You hit him in the solar plexus with that thang he'll
probably just git up and run away.'

'They'll have heard that racket,' Howling Wolf
cried. 'We better vamoose.'

'Yeah, too true.' The Texan swung onto the quarter-horse and sat straight-backed, a carbine in the
boot, a .45 in the holster of an ammunition belt,
another in his saddle-bag, a knife in his belt. He was
ready for them now. He kneed the horse forward and
it strode away with a powerful springing gait. He
turned it and watched Lucy struggling to climb onto
a mustang. 'Come on, Luce,' he shouted. 'You gotta
try to keep up.'

As he and Howling Wolf spurted away towards the
town she climbed aboard, and, one hand hanging on
the horn, went bouncing away after them. 'Wait for
me, you bastards,' she yelled.

They rode at a fast lope along the ravine towards
the oncoming railroad for about a mile until the
Wichita held up his hand for them to halt. His sharp
eyes had spotted a dust spiral up ahead. He jumped
down and put his ear to the ground. 'Old Indian
trick.' He flashed a grin. 'Big bunch of riders coming
. . . twenty or thirty of 'em.'

They moved their horses up behind some huge
boulders at the foot of the cliff wall and took cover.
The posse of men came pounding towards them led
by Sheriff Lipcott, Casper and a thin dude, nattily
dressed beneath his duster coat and tall hat. The
deputy Joe, the remains of Casper's hard men, and a
motley crew of townsmen and ranch-hands, gathered
in their wake.

'That must be Frank Canton,' the Texan said.

'Heard tell he sports them Chinee whiskers. Pity I ain't got my Creedmore. I coulda blasted him outa the saddle. They're out of range for this durn carbine.'

'What's he doing here?' Lucy exclaimed as she watched them flash by.

'Maybe the marshal didn't git your cable.'

'You mean it was intercepted?' she stared at him, distraught. 'That means we're cut off. Washington, New York, nobody knows my side of the story.'

'Waal,' he drawled, 'while they're outa the way we could make a dash for Fort Arbuckle. Or up the railroad to Guthrie, explain what's goin' on to the authorities. Or you could. I don't figure they'd be interested in listenin' to me. What's it gonna be? Run or fight? It's make your mind up time.'

As they made their way back to the bottom of the ravine there were muffled reverberations at the digging site, and a column of smoke and dust rose into the air. 'Looks like they're havin' fun,' Howling Wolf shouted. 'Blowin' up your bones, burnin' the tents and stores to let us know they've called.'

'They're askin' fer trouble,' the Texan muttered.

Lucy blinked away tears that spurted to her eyes. 'How can they? The vandals!'

'I asked you a question.'

She stared at him, angrily. 'Fight!'

'Come on.' He spurred his horse forward and led them climbing up through the mountains. They stood poised on a crest looking down the steep descent. His horse shied as another explosion sent up a shower of rocks down below. The railroad crew were making good progress, working like frantic ants to shovel earth and rocks for the railroad bed, build trestle bridges, and blast tunnels through solid rock. The snaking line of their route to the crest had already been marked out with staves, slashed through a stand of pines. 'They ain't hangin' about,' he said.

They followed the proposed route down and when they reached the workers he raised his revolver and yelled, 'Charge!'

Lucy gripped her Mauser, gritted her teeth, and spurred her mustang hard to try to catch up with them as they went galloping away. The Texan was giving a weird, keening Rebel yell, and the Indian screaming his death chant, as they went charging at the labourers, firing over their heads, sending them scrambling out of the way. An Irishman raised his pickaxe to hurl at Pete's horse, but Howling Wolf's lead hammered into his shoulder before he could throw. Lucy was swept on after them and could not avoid a sense of exhilaration as she fired off the Mauser. Was this why men loved war so?

The Texan did not stop but led them on along the completed rails towards the sheds and bivouacs of the workers' camp. The ruddy-faced clerk of works saw them coming and ran, his body wobbling in his baggy check suit, back towards the steaming locomotive and the big crane. As he tried to climb aboard, Pete's lariat landed over his shoulders and jerked him bouncing away among the dust and flints. He dragged him for a hundred paces, then turned and hauled him back. Harry Jones looked up fearfully, his loud suit torn and bloodstained by the sharp flints.

'Where you keep the dynamite?' the Texan shouted.

The foreman scrambled up, reaching for his keys.

'Over in the cabin. Don't shoot! Take as much as you want.'

'I intend to.' He sat his horse and gave the rope a jerk as the man tried to remove it from his corpulent body. 'Jest git that door opened.'

Lucy kept the engineer and fireman covered, beckoning them to step down, and Howling Wolf brandished his big old Dragoon at other workers, telling them to back off. He got hold of a mule and some rope as the Texan emerged from the cabin with boxes of dynamite. They loaded it onto the wooden saddle.

'Need some fuses and wire,' Pete growled, and when these were produced, swung back onto his patch horse. 'You,' he said, aiming his revolver at the foreman. 'I see you again I'll kill you. I suggest you git the first train outa this town back to where you come from, find some other job. And you other varmints, too. This railroad ain't goin' nowhere. You keep diggin' into this mountain you'll be diggin' your own graves. I'm givin' you fair warning.'

He wheeled his horse and dragged the clerk of works tumbling and bouncing along the track for a bit. He let him stagger up, remove the rope from around his shoulders, and, as he slowly wound it, shouted, 'All you others better wise up. It ain't gonna be safe to work for James Casper.'

Silent and sullen, Jones and the others stood and watched them as they ambled away along the track, the Indian leading the mule.

'I got a feeling he's not joking,' the engineer said.

They cantered into Sulphur Springs, guns holstered, but alert, passing through the sprinkling of farmers, shoppers, Indians and idlers, who paid them little heed. They dismounted outside the law office and jail, and the Texan raised his boot to kick at the door, but it was solidly locked. By now people had begun to stop and watch him. He calmly took a stick of dynamite from his coat pocket and lit the fuse end with his smoking cheroot. He got back on his horse and moved away. He tossed the dynamite and the jail door was blitzed open.

'They're breaking into the sheriff's office!' someone shouted, and men came running. Howling Wolf deterred them, whanging lead whistling past their heads from his carbine. And Lucy decided to get in some practice with her Mauser, too, trying not to kill anyone.

The whiskey-fuelled mob that had once tried to string her and the Texan up by their necks were not so brave when faced by three armed and dangerous desperadoes in the sober light of day, with the sheriff's posse out of town. They watched from a safe distance, curiously, as the Texan swung down and stepped over the fallen doors into the smoke and rubble.

'What in hail's goin' on?' a drunk wailed as he peered through the bars. 'You come to rescue me?'

Black Pete ignored him, looking around for the strong box he had seen the sheriff stuff his papers into. He drew his revolver and blasted the lock apart. He took out a sheaf of cash and counted out $500 of Lucy's and $170-odd of his own.

'You tell the sheriff I called for the cash he stole from me and from my friend when he wrongfully arrested her. And I'll have my Creedmore while I'm here.' He took it from the rack, fondly, checking it was primed, and looked in the desk drawers. 'My Smith & Wesson, too.' He stuck the other revolver in his belt and slid the .44 into his thigh holster, slapping it. 'That feels better. So long, *hombre.*'

A shot clapped out, splintering the sidewalk post as he emerged, and he saw a man crouched at the open doorway of the tinware store. The .44 came out like greased lightning, and he levered out a slug, arm outstretched. The man tumbled back clattering and clanging into his own piles of hardware.

'There's allus got to be a hero,' he growled, eyes narrowed, revolver at the ready, glancing around.

Two other men had taken up positions behind a water butt, taking pot-shots at them, and he and Henry sent them dodging back into the sidestreets pursued by their lead.

Pete stuffed the Creedmore into the saddle holster, swung up onto his bronc and spurted down the dusty street, leaping the heavy horse onto the wooden sidewalk, scattering baskets of produce. Ducking his head, he rode him into the Wild Cat Saloon. Girls screamed and scrambled out of the way of his hooves, and card players were knocked aside like skittles as he plunged the whinnying, rearing horse through them, wheeling around, and firing his revolver, crashing and whistling bullets over the heads of anyone who looked like giving him trouble.

'Gimme a couple bottles of that whiskey,' he shouted at the brawny-armed barkeep, waving his gun at the shelf. The 'keep quickly did so, tossing one to him, which he caught left-handed, and stuck in his suit pocket. He pulled the cork of the next with his teeth and took a pull. 'That's the stuff,' he gasped.

He grinned, recorked his bottle, and stuck it in his belt. 'Tell Casper and Canton I'll be waitin' for 'em.' He whirled the quarter-horse around like a circus animal, doffing its white mane, and rode out. Lucy and Henry were waiting, covering the street. But the citizens had decided it unwise to intervene. They just stood and stared as the three 'outlaws' loosed off the last shots in their revolvers at hanging hurricane lamps and shop signs and rode at a fast clip out of town, trailing their mule.

Eleven

Bret Spalding had proposed to Casper that he stay behind to keep an eye on the town while the posse went in search of the Texan. When they were gone he rode out towards the Littlejohn's farm. He hitched his horse beneath some cottonwoods on the far side of the corral from the cabin and stables. All was quiet, an old grey mare, and a couple of mustangs tossing some hay in a corner of the corral, smoke lazily rising from the cabin chimney. A little girl, with a rag doll in one hand, was playing in the dust outside. Her mother's voice called pleasantly, 'Bess, come inside for your lunch.'

'Yeah, me, too,' Bret said, smiling to himself. He watched the toddler go indoors and crept quietly around the corral, loosening the revolver in his holster. The cabin windows were smashed, its log walls pocked with bullet holes. He went round the back and, through a window, glimpsed the fair hair of the nineteen-year-old girl, saw her soft cheeks and tilted nose in profile as she bent over a stove in the kitchen area of the two-roomed house. There was a scent of stew curling through the broken window. 'That smells real nice,' he murmured.

He stepped up onto the veranda and through the

118

smashed-in front door. He glanced in the other room and saw a baby in a papoose-board on the bed. The curly-haired little girl stared at him with wide blue eyes. He looked at her and put a finger to his lips. Her mother had her back to him, unsuspecting, humming some melody as she stirred at the pot. She screamed as he put his muscular arms around her.

'Surprise,' he whispered, gagging her with a hand. 'Guess who it ain't?'

'You leave my mommy 'lone,' the little girl blurted out.

'Go in the other room, kid.'

'Bess!' Judy said. 'Do as he says. Go on. Shut the door.'

'Thass right,' Bret grinned, stroking her cheek and neck with his thick fingers. 'We don' wan' her seein' what she didn' oughta see at her age.' He watched as the child did as she was bid. 'Shut it, kid. Me an' your mommy's got a date with destiny.'

Judy froze as his fingers groped at her breasts beneath her dress, his tongue licked, insidiously, at her ear, and she heard his thick-lipped voice. 'I allus had my eye on you. Why you throw yourself away on that stinkin' Injin? I bin waitin' to git in your li'l stew-pot a long time. You play your cards right, Judy, nobody ain't gonna git hurt. You gonna find out what a real man's like, a white man.'

'Please, don't, Bret,' she whispered. 'Henry's my only man. We was married in church. Don't do this. Why don't you leave us alone?'

'You an' me gonna git acquainted.' He grinned, tossed his hat away, holding her by the waist. 'We're gonna—'

'Don't!' She swung away from him, hurling the pot

of scalding stew in his face. As he cursed and groped, half-blinded, she snatched up the kitchen knife and thrust it at him, stabbing it into his upper arm.

'You bitch,' he howled, grabbing her wrist, twisting the knife free. The girl slipped past, and dashed out into the yard. He wiped most of the hot mess from his face and hair and staggered after her, looking with horror at the blood beginning to matt his shirt arm. 'You'll pay for that,' he roared, but she had disappeared.

Judy stood, her heart thudding, inside the shadow of the barn doorway. She wanted to draw him away from her children. She wanted to escape. She knew Bret Spalding was just as likely to kill her, kill her children once he had had his way. She glanced desperately around but the stalls were empty. The horses were in the corral. There was no other way out. 'I'm going to get you,' she heard him shouting, in a sing-song, as he walked across the yard, nearer, and nearer. Her gaze fell on a pitch-fork and she reached out for it. She saw his big-shouldered shadow as he stood in the doorway, looking in. 'Where a-r-e you?'

It was his turn to scream as the slim girl whirled out before him and speared the pitchfork into his face. One prong bounced off the bone of his broken nose and out through the side of his cheek. 'Agh!' he cried, getting hold of the fork handle and dragging it from her, tossing it clattering away. As she tried to slip past him he caught her by her dress which ripped apart, and by her thick, corn-coloured hair. 'Try to blind me, would you?'

In a livid rage he smashed her in the face with his fist. The impact made her teeth cut deep into her lip. She fell back on the ground, dazed, looking up, her mouth trickling blood. She tried to scramble away, but the bloody-faced man, roaring obscenities, bull-angry, dragged her up by her hair, and smashed his fist into her eyes.

'You want any more, you wildcat?' He was breathing hard, He tumbled over her, a knee between her legs, her wrists held in one huge hand, the other poised to fist her again. 'I'll kill you.'

His heavy shoulders slumped down upon her, almost suffocating her, as he tore at her dress, at her underwear, hauling her thighs up over his shoulders, fumbling and thrusting at her. Judy groaned and succumbed, and she felt a searing pain as he entered her. There was little more she could do. Bret gasped for breath as his blood and sweat dripped onto her face, and she cried out, 'No . . . oh . . . oh!' as her spreadeagled fingers gripped the dust.

'I bet you ain't had it like that,' he said, some while later, as he collapsed upon her.

That was the understatement of the year, she thought, as bruised and torn, hating his stink, his strength, his bullish redolence, she croaked out, 'Bret . . . don't do nuthin' . . . my kids . . . I ain't gonna tell no one.'

'You bet you aint, you bitch,' he grinned down at her, raising himself on his powerful arms – and then he suddenly shot his arms out, his head snapping back, and he fell upon her, flailing with his hands, seeking the arrow that had pierced his back, the arrow that had gone clean through his rib cage.

Judy could feel the point pricking against her chest, and she thrust him, rolling off, still kicking, twisting, groaning, his face contorted in agony as he tried to catch hold of the feathered shaft. She stared at him and whispered, 'Gosh! What a way to go!'

And then up at her husband, who, in his fringed jacket, leggings and headband, was standing there, bow in hand, staring at them. 'You've killed him.'

'You bet your sweet life I have. I could hardly believe my eyes when I saw him and you down in the dust of the yard going at it like that.'

'He made me,' she screamed, for some reason of modesty trying to cover herself with the torn dress. 'I fought him. Look at his face!'

Howling Wolf rolled the big man over with his moccasinned foot. 'Yeah, it looks like you did. Only, at first, I thought . . .'

'Please don't be like this.'

'I'm sorry,' he said, kneeling to hold her as she sobbed and shook against his chest. 'It looks like I got here a few minutes too late.'

'Daddy,' the little girl called, peeping from the window where she had climbed. 'What's wrong with mommy? Why's she crying?'

'Hang on, honey,' he said. 'Mommy's fine.'

He helped her to her feet, gently washed her face at the horse trough. He turned and looked at the prostrate Spalding. 'I think we better get out of here. Nobody will believe us.'

'Where will we go?' she whimpered. 'What about the chickens, the cows?'

'We got to think of our own lives. I'll harness the wagon. You head south-east towards Tishomingo. It's the capital of Choctaw Territory. You'll be safe there.'

'What will you do, Henry?'

'I go fight with Pete.'

'No, please, I need you.'

'I'm a warrior. I have to.'

*

'Here's to the greatest benefactor of mankind.' The Texan raised the bottle and reclined on a bed of pine boughs to ease his ageing limbs. 'The man who brought us Southerners comfort and joy.'

'Who's he?'

'The Rev Elijah Craig, inventor of bourbon whiskey. In Bourbon, Kentucky, 1789. I got a lot of useless knowledge in my head, jest like you and Henry.'

Lucy Luffy watched him, anxiously, as he took a good gulp of the first bottle. 'You're not planning on getting drunk again?'

'Nope, jest warming the cockles of my heart, as they say. Why don't you come over here an' warm it with me?'

'You seem to be doing OK without me.' Already his speech was getting slurred, and he was waving the bottle about, grandly. After the Wichita had left them, they had returned by a devious route to this cavern where the night before she and he . . . but she regretted that already. 'What is it with you drinkers? Do you enter another world? Why do you suddenly become so verbose?'

'Why don't you try a drop?' He proffered the bottle. 'Find out for yourself.'

'One of us has to stay sober. What if they follow us?'

'Aw, by the time they git back from their chase they'll be too tired an' weary. Come on, relax.'

They had dined on antelope, roasted in the embers, Indian fashion. When he sliced the doe open he found she was pregnant, with a small fawn inside her. It had touched her, the way he had apologized to the animal. 'I wouldn't have shot you if I'd known,' he had said.

Lucy could not bring herself to eat the fawn, as he did. 'It's real toothsome,' he had laughed. 'Injins regard it as a great delicacy.' Nonetheless, the mother was very tasty. She had almost devoured a whole leg, she was so hungry.

How could a man be so gentle, so tender hearted, and so hard and callous, at the same time? And, to cap it all, be a boorish slave to whiskey? How could she want such a man, a killer and outlaw?

'I don't want to lie down over there,' she excused herself, acidly. 'I don't like those nasty little caterpillars on the pine needles.'

'Aw, they won't hurt you. Come on, cowboy, take a slug.'

She gave a brief smile at his reference to her get-up. Admittedly, it made her feel strange. Nor would she have believed, three days before, that she would have been gallivanting around the countryside, open-legged on a mustang, dressed so, firing a lethal weapon at the population. But the memory of the news story, the lies, the way they had tried to frame her, hang her, still rankled. It juddered back into her like a stab of lightning. She had never believed she could be so grossly insulted. The humiliation had stung her like a whiplash. And all this man could do was sprawl out, indecently, with a bottle in his hand, expecting her to jump into his arms.

'C'mon, Lucy, what's wrong? Why you so down in the dumps?'

'It's all right for you. You don't give a tinker's cuss. You're like all the others. You hold life so cheap. Your morals are so lax. You don't seem to care what happens to you. But I've been brought up differently. I've no wish to be branded as a murderer, to be accused of such conduct. Last night, I'm sorry, it was a mistake. I was grateful to you. I was in a state of shock. But I've no wish to be regarded as some outlaw's whore. What if that news-sheet is sent East? How can I prevent such calumnies being repeated in the national journals?'

'I dunno,' he muttered, moodily. 'I can see what you're grieving at. But, surely, nobody's gonna believe that bull—'

'People believe what they read. You said so.'

'Guess you got a point.' He tipped the bottle to his mouth. 'Me, I'm past caring what anyone thinks. But you, yes, it ain't right. So, it was jest like a one-night thang?'

'No.' She shook her head haughtily at such an idea. 'But, what if I became pregnant? Don't you see? I can't risk it. I don't have any birth control.'

'Only control I know is whip-it-out-quick.'

'Really!' She could not help being offended by him. She was not used to being spoken to in such a manner. 'Sometimes you appal me. You're so flippant about life.'

'Yeah? Waal, if we ain't gonna have no fun guess I better clean my gun. You better clean yours, too. We don't wanna git flippant about our chances of stayin' alive.'

In spite of being in an obvious state of shock, Judy had insisted on piling what few belongings they had, pots and pans, milk churns, wooden chests and chairs, onto the wagon. To please her, Henry had caught a few of the fowls, stuffed them, squawking, into wire-meshed crates, and tied their two cows behind. But he dissuaded her from piling their bed on top. 'We got to make time,' he said, as she tottered in and out from the cabin with bric-à-brac. He harnessed the grey mare, the two mustangs, and Spalding's sorrel to the wagon. Four-horse power was better than one. The cows would just have to try to keep up – Judy claimed she needed them for the baby's milk. He hoisted a big barrel aboard and filled it with water – it was a long journey.

The young Indian dragged Spalding's cumbersome body into the woods and stripped it of identifying objects, giving Judy his billfold and a thick gold ring. 'Keep this cash for emergencies in case – just in case. He owed it us.' His clothes he tossed on the fire and his revolver, the Hopkins and Allan .36, he told his wife to carry with the shotgun. 'If anybody pesters you, kill 'em. Get your shot in first. Don't wait to ask questions.'

They waited until dusk before rattling away. The wolves, bears or foxes would soon make short work of Spalding's body, and serve him right. They gave the town a wide berth and abandoned the railroad to take the winding trail around to the digging site. Fortunately there was a full moon casting a bright glow, almost as light as day, reflected off the silver-grey granite outcrops. 'What we stopping here for now?' Judy asked.

'You gotta give me a hand to get those two crates of mammoth tusks and artefacts on the wagon,' he said, leading the way across to the stand of pines. 'Thank the God of Thunder those white fools did not find them. These belong to us, to the Chickasaw nation and the Washita tribe.'

When they had hefted them onto the back of the wagon, and covered them with tarpaulin, he instructed: 'Take these to Tishomingo to the chief's house. Tell him we will open our own museum of our native history to let people know who we were, what we were like, before they wipe us all out. Why should they go to New York to be paraded before the ignorant savage whites? This is their spiritual home.'

'I only hope you know what you're doin', Henry,' she said.

He looked at her with tears in his eyes. She had such a fragile and determined air, sitting on the box of the wagon, ready to go, one eye bloody, almost closed, a lump of blue swelling growing fast, a tooth broken, her lips puffy and torn, damaged and shamed in body, but still resilient, and strong in heart. 'You have given me great happiness as my wife,' he said. 'If I die in battle do not grieve too much. We will meet again in the afterworld.' He reached over and fondled Bess's fair hair.

'Take care,' Judy called, although she knew he would not, for he was wild and reckless. 'Carry our love with you.'

She flicked the reins and they rumbled away. She had a vague idea of the way for they had visited his tribe on the Washita, and once they reached that river it would be easier. She would travel all night guided by the stars.

Henry sat his spotted stallion and watched them disappear, saw his little daughter turn to wave, and, flicking the tears from his eyes, turned his horse back to look for Pete and his woman. To fight.

Twelve

The Flyer, with its bell clanging above the cowcatcher, and its tall stack shooting out a column of black smoke, came hushing and shushing, groaning and wheezing, slowing into Sulphur Springs. A long, lean ash-blond man, dressed like a funeral director in a bowstring tie and black frock coat, stepped down and gave the town a lookover with eyes bright and glittering from consumption. He carried a black silk plug hat in one hand, a burning cheroot in his fingers, and a carpet bag in the other, which rattled ominously as he set it down.

'Where's James Casper hang out?' he asked the railroad clerk in a throaty whisper.

'Over in the Wild Cat Saloon.'

He strolled over, and, on entering, glanced about, checking the occupants, as was his custom, the custom of all who lived by the gun. Nothing much to concern him. Just a few deadbeats and dingoes at the gaming tables, or playing cards, some squawking waiter girls, a professor of piano on the pode tinkling a tune.

'Gimme a bottle of the best,' he hissed at the brawny barman, who was heavy-bearded, in a lumberjack shirt. 'No, not that filth. You call that best. Ain't you got no bourbon?'

'Who the hell are you?'

'I've come to see Casper. Tell him his troubles are over. The dentist is here.'

'The only bourbon we got is up in his room.'

'Tell him to bring it down. And dang quick.'

There was something about the man's glittering stare that made the barman act quick. He got on the telephone intercom, wound the battery and spoke into the mouthpiece. 'You got your dentist down here, suh. You got a bad tooth?'

'I ain't interested in his oral hygiene. Tell him to git his ass down here pronto. I'll be sittin' over yonder.'

'He wants you to bring down your bourbon, pronto, Mistuh Casper. No, he ain't the sort of man I aim to argue with.'

The dentist settled himself down in a corner chair and swung open his frock coat to reveal an eight-inch slim-barrelled Frontier single action, engraved with gold and silver inlay, a silver Colt-rampant insignia on the smooth walnut butt. It was held securely in a scabbard of chased leather attached to his belt. Like most gamblers, he carried a two-shot derringer inside his coat, and an 'eye-gouger' in his boot. He watched Casper emerge onto the balcony, a bottle in his hands, followed by Frank Canton.

'Doctor Holliday?' James Casper said, as he approached. 'This is a great pleasure. Your reputation is legendary and precedes you.'

'Cut the crap. Just give me the booze. The name's Doc.' He reached out for the bourbon and poured himself a tumbler-full. He tasted it and sighed, wiping a finger across his thick blond moustache. 'At least, you stock decent whiskey.' He eyed Canton, malevolently. 'What's that grasshopper's fart doin' here?'

'The marshal is working for me.'

'Marshal? Hech! That what he calls himself?' Holliday drew thirstily on the bourbon. 'What's the griff?'

'To kill two outlaws. A Texan called Bowen and his Indian sidekick. That you do by whatever means possible. There is a young woman, Miss Lucy Luffy, who has East coast connections, senators and so forth. She must be erased, if possible, more discreetly.'

'If she's riding with these bandits, and if she's charged with murder, anyway, I don't see—' Frank Canton began.

'A phoney rap, eh?' Holliday cut in. 'You don't need this idjit. I'm the operator for you. I clean up after me.'

'No. I have to make sure of this. I'm in a hurry. I can afford the both of you. How much do you want, or should we discuss that privately?'

'Five hundred more than you're payin' this lick-spittle so-called marshal.'

Canton's grey eyes were stone still as he stared at him. 'You'd better be careful what you say, mister, or you won't just be *spittin'* blood.'

Holliday had suddenly become wracked with coughing, clutching his chest, his whole fragile frame convulsed. He reached for his handkerchief and spotted it with scarlet. The tubercular germs had already taken up residence in both of his lungs. It was obvious that at thirty-four he did not have many years left. He would have been lucky to make thirty-five.

Canton watched him, contemptuously. 'He gets the same as me.'

Holliday recovered himself, somewhat. 'OK,' he growled, 'but I need all the bourbon I can drink. That a deal?'

James Casper looked a mite uneasy. This man, a former 'sidesman' of Wyatt Earp, was supposed to be reknowned as the nerviest, speediest, deadliest man with a six-gun ever to roam the West. And it was matched only by his dedication and skill at poker and other games of chance. But it struck him that might well have been in the past. However, he took out his wallet and lay down several crisp large denomination notes, a fortune to anyone else. 'I'm paying one thousand two hundred and fifty dollars for the three. There's six hundred dollars down, the rest on completion.'

Holliday had another fit of coughing as he tried to pick up the money. 'Excuse me,' he gasped. 'Whiskey went down the wrong way.'

Canton gave a hollow laugh. 'He's started making excuses already. What good's this gutter rat? Look at his fingers shaking. I doubt if he can even aim a gun.'

Holliday looked up at him over the 'kerchief pressed to his mouth, his eyes baleful. 'I best not hear you say that once I got a bottle of this Kentucky down me.'

'Gentlemen,' Casper intervened. 'I'm not paying you to fight among yourselves. You must work together. Arrange a plan.'

'A plan?' Holliday said. 'I suggest long-shanks there protects your railroad. I'll cover the town. If he shows his nose here I'll kill him, an' the other two, legal or otherwise, I don't care.'

'Suits me,' Canton said. 'The less I have to do with this specimen of humanity the better. I've come across better things under stones.'

Holliday laughed, caustically. 'The marshal's gittin' prissy. Who is this Bowen? I never heard of him.'

'He is not much known. A wanderer, a loner. I understand he has been down in Mexico fighting for Villa. Some call him Black Pete. You will know him when you see him. I warn you, he is not a man to underestimate.'

'Boss.' The barkeep touched his sleeve. 'Bret Spalding's disappeared. He was seen riding out to the Littlejohn's farm.'

'Come to think of it,' Casper said, 'neither is that Indian sidekick of his.'

'Sure. You frighten me.' Holliday took a pack of cards from his pocket and idly flicked through them, spreading them out across the table, and picking them up again, as if magnetically, his fingers as nimble as a magician's. 'So, you boys? You ready to lose some money?'

They looked like two innocent babes when Howling Wolf got back to the cave at two in the morning. They were lying on the pine-brush bed, Lucy rolled over, her head rested on his arm, both peacefully sleeping.

'What you doin' here?' The Texan woke with a start from his whiskey slumber, jerking his .44 out from beneath the blanket. 'Howja manage to creep up on me like that?'

'Because I'm a pesky Indian, thass why.' Henry grinned as Lucy awoke and, rather primly, moved away from the outlaw. 'I gotta tell you something,

Miss Luffy. I've taken your crates of mammoth tusks and stuff.'

'What?' she exclaimed. 'What are you talking about?'

'Your finds. I have repossessed them on behalf of the Chickasaw tribal government. They are being transported to Tishomingo.'

'How dare you? Those finds belong to the late Dr Stares and myself, and the New York Scientific Union. Who gave you the right to purloin them?'

'The Chickasaw Tribe self-governs this Territory,' Pete chuckled. 'They got the right.'

'Yes, we still have some rights that haven't been whittled away,' Howling Wolf said. 'Don't worry, Miss Luffy. The artefacts will be jealousy guarded in our tribal museum . . . I hope.'

'You hope.' She sat up, trying to straighten her hair and her shirt, and frowned at them. And then she smiled. 'That's all right, Henry. In some ways it's a relief. Perhaps you have done the right thing. So, we have no need to fight any more. We can go our separate ways. It's all over.'

'No, it's not over,' Howling Wolf said. 'If you made these important finds in that ravine there must be a hidden village nearby, say a mile or so away from their hunting pit. They would need to be near to their source of meat. That valley may yield marvellous things. We must not let the railroad desecrate it. We have a lot of work to do there, both you and me.'

'You mean the fight's still on?' Pete groaned.

'Looks like it,' Lucy smiled.

'If we die in battle it is good,' Howling Wolf told Lucy as he sharpened the iron points of his arrows. He had

Rogue Railroad

fashioned them from pieces of a barrel hoop. The bow he had made from yew, three feet six inches in length, painted ochre and green. The twelve arrows in his quiver were two feet long and winged with hawk feathers, and made from a semi-poisonous greasewood. 'It is good to die for our rights, to die fighting for this country.'

They had taken their stand on the rim of Windy Ridge, looking down at the winding course of the railroad that was almost to the peak. Lucy wished the Wichita would not keep talking about dying. It made her stomach queasy. She had no wish to give up her studies just yet. But she supposed it was a possibility, quite a strong one, that she might not see another dawn. Or that she might have to shoot to kill if she wanted to stay alive.

She crouched down, her blanket around her shoulders, as she watched the blood-red sun rise, and far below them the Texan on his horse making preparations to kill not just one but many men. He had packed with dynamite three empty oil drums discarded by the railroad crew, and was busy concealing them at varying points beneath the iron rails, attaching fuses and detonators. He had learned how to dispense death with explosives during guerilla raids in the Civil War at the tender age of sixteen. It was as if his experiences in that dreadful holocaust had made him hardened, cynical, immune to mass suffering. Not for the first time, Lucy wondered what madness had made her ride with these two.

She shivered as the bitterly cold wind that always strafed the ridge cut through her. The Wichita was stripping his buckskin coat and shirt off, ready for battle, his bronzed arms braceleted, a bear-tooth necklace around his throat, his darkly muscled, rib-thin body painted with magic signs. He seemed impervious to cold, his mind willed into a higher state. He had hidden his carbine, revolver and ammunition belt beneath a rock.

'You're not planning to fight their guns with that primitive bow?' she said.

He grinned at her, proudly, through hair that was whipped across his face by the wind. 'This is how Washita fight.'

Lucy was tense as she waited. She had only the lightweight Mauser against experienced, heavily armed shootists. They had told her to stay back, to hang on to the horses, which would be startled by the noise of battle. 'How do you know they will come?'

'They will be coming,' he said.

And, sure enough, as the sun climbed higher, she saw a column of smoke shoot into the sky as the Katie engine was stoked up, and began to move towards them. She used the Texan's brass telescope to peer at it for it was still a good distance off, but beginning to climb fast up the curving track, huffing and puffing. The sun glinted on the rifles and carbines of men leaned from the windows of the two carriages. She counted about thirty of them. James Casper must have hired more men, or else they had volunteered for the posse. Three against thirty. What chance had they got? She licked her lips, nervously, as she began to feel like a hunted fox with the hounds baying at her den.

She focused the telescope with some difficulty and suddenly caught the Texan in its lens. He was lying down in a gully about half a mile in front of the approaching engine as it came chugging around the bends. He was calmly smoking a cheroot. No! He appeared to be lighting a fuse. He got to his feet and ran to swing onto his quarter-horse and set off up the track. A quarter of a mile on he swung down and kneeled to light another fuse. He climbed onto the powerful horse and pounded on up the steep slope.

Lucy lay the 'scope aside as he climbed nearer. He was about 200 yards away below them and she could hear the harsh panting of his horse as it struggled up the ascent. He halted and climbed down again, took his Creedmore from the saddle-boot, and steadied it on top of a boulder. As he did so the engine passed over the first can of dynamite. Perhaps he had miscalculated? Perhaps the fuse was too long, or had fizzed out? But, suddenly, the rear carriage and guard's van of the train erupted in a flash of fire, with a muffled roar, and there was a pyrotechnic display as bits of bodies, carriage, rails and earth were showered into the sky.

There were hoarse shouts as men jumped from the remains of the carriage, scrambling away, one of them on fire, rolling in the dust. The van and carriage had keeled over and it was amazing that anyone had survived. But other men had stepped down from the first carriage, running, turning to see what had occurred.

The Texan levered the Creedmore and sighted along the solid barrel. A shot coughed out, and, before its echo had ceased barrelling off the mountain wall, its heavyweight bullet ploughed into a man's back and out through his chest. He levered another slug into the breech, squeezed it out and another man bit the dust.

'They was warned,' he gritted out to himself, as

others of the posse dived for cover. He saw the bulky shape of Sheriff Hank Lipcott waving his arms and shouting. He aimed, fired, but missed. Perhaps he had misjudged the gusting power of the wind on that ridge. Still, two out of three, at over three quarters of a mile wasn't bad shooting.

The men had retreated behind the train and were either clearing rubble, disconnecting the remains of the rear carriage, or seeing to the injured. However, the engine spurted smoke and, towing the first carriage, started up the slope again. They had waited longer than he had anticipated, and it was unlikely the second can of explosive would do much damage. But no, on and on and on they came, faster and faster, winding around a solid wall of rock, and through a short tunnel, and back into sight and – Pow! – the rails were mangled and a fountain of rocks flew up just before the engine reached that spot. Unable to be stopped in time, the sturdy little 'iron horse' ploughed off the rails and down the mountainside, the carriage slipping over and sliding down behind it, almost in slow motion, the two jack-knifing to a halt.

Black Pete left his horse behind the boulder and dodged back down to the third can packed with explosives. He struck a match on the serrated edge of his silver match case and carefully lit the fuse, blowing on it to get it going. He climbed back up to his big horse and holstered the Creedmore, getting a foot in the bentwood stirrup and swinging into the saddle as the horse went prancing away up the track until it reached its end. Then he spurred it on up through the blazed boulders and trees and red earth.

'There he is!' a voice shouted as men jumped from

the windows of the wrecked train.

Rifles and carbines began to crack and bullets buzzed about his head as the Texan reached the base of the granite cliff beneath the topmost peak of the ridge where his friends were concealed. He wheeled the quarter-horse round to take a look.

Sheriff Hank Lipcott was standing beside young James Casper, and was brandishing his carbine, urging what men he had left forward. About twenty of them were running up the incline towards the Texan, blamming away with revovlers. A taller, slim man, in a bowl-shaped hat stepped out from behind the overturned carriage. The Texan saw his thin Mongolian moustache – Frank Canton. He had a rifle at his shoulder. There was a crack of the report, a puff of smoke, and shards of granite were chiselled from the rock face into his eyes as the slug whistled past his cheek. This was shooting of a different order.

For moments he was at a loss what to do. Whether to drag his horse up through scrub and boulders of the steep incline to join his friends? Or to stand and face them? The third can had yet to explode. Could his famed judgement have abandoned him? He was certainly in a tight spot. Canton's second bullet nearly took his hat off, ripping through the brim. He ducked, instinctively, as the lead of the advancing men buzzed about him like angry bees.

There was a roar and a ruddy flash as his third bomb went up under the feet of those in front, blowing them to atoms, bits and pieces of flesh and blood mingled with flying rocks, the blast hurling others off their feet.

As the dust settled there was an uncanny silence, broken only by the moans of the injured. There were

about eight or nine men left standing. Pete decided
to take the battle to them, but, as he climbed on his
horse, stood in the stirrups, raised his revolver and
charged, he saw the determined figure of Canton
with the rifle at his shoulder further down the track.
He heard the whistle of the bullet, his horse's scream
as the rifled slug tore and twisted into its chest, felt
the knees buckle, saw the head and forequarters
going down, and he was flung with a body-sickening
crunch to the ground. He tried to roll clear, but too
late, his leg was trapped and crushed.

'I got him,' Canton breathed out with great satis-
faction, lowering his rifle. 'One lousy Texan Reb
de-horsed. You can pay me the rest of my fee right
now.'

'Hang on,' Lipcott shouted. 'It ain't over yet. That
redskin'll be around some place.' As his men raced
up the hill to claim the Texan and finish him, the
sheriff crouched down, scanning the cliff, his carbine
raised in readiness.

T-zit! An arrow hissed from behind a boulder and
the leading runner threw up his arms as it pierced his
chest. T-zit! The gun-toting man behind him fell
back, an arrow stuck in his forehead.

The rest of the gunmen were nearly upon the
fallen Texan when the Wichita showed himself, his
arms raised, screaming his battle chant, a scalping
knife in his hand. As Hank Lipcott blammed his
carbine at him he leaped from the clifftop, bounding
from stone to stone like a deer, and with a final
mighty jump of some fifteen feet landed on the
shoulders of the running men, knocking them aside
like fallen apples.

Howling Wolf slashed at two throats and was back

up on his feet. A man on one knee was pointing a carbine at him. He wrestled him for the gun, and, simultaneously, gashed his head open. Two men were running towards him. He hurled the carbine at them and leapt, knocking them aside. They hardly stopped him a second before he plunged his knife into the abdomen of a sixth man.

The Wichita paused when he saw Canton, Casper, and Lipcott fifty yards away down the track, their weapons aimed at him. He froze on the balls of his feet, and leaped aside as their shots rattled out. He decided discretion was better than suicide, and turned in his tracks, running back towards his fallen friend, dodging and leaping like a crazed mountain lion from side to side.

'Why don't he stay still?' Lipcott moaned, and began dodging back for the cover of the train, himself, as a shot from a carbine snarled into the dust too close for comfort. And a second and third made Casper and Canton join him. 'There's someone up on top of the cliff.'

'He's got us covered,' Canton said, as he peered out and snapped off a quick rifle shot.

'Or she.' Casper looked around him, his face agitated. 'We're the last ones left. They've killed every damn one of our men. Talk about the fighters from hell. What can we do? I've an idea that might be that Luffy hussy up there. But she seems to know how to shoot.'

'No way we're gonna git up that open space,' Lipcott said. 'Not with the luck we're having.'

Howling Wolf had reached the Texan and had somehow managed to free his leg from beneath the dead quarter-horse. Canton peered out and saw

Bowen hobble away behind a rock, his arm around the Indian's bare shoulders. 'Shee-it!' he whistled, as another bullet splintered into the carriage near his head. 'I hate to see 'em get away.'

'There'll be another day,' Casper said.

None of the three men felt inclined to go after their attackers, not without back-up. And they glimpsed the figure of the Indian on a spotted horse, followed by another bronc with two-up, moving away over the crest. Canton stepped out, but the bullet whistled from his rifle futilely. They had gone. All they could do was turn back and count the cost.

Thirteen

Doc Holliday's head ached like it had been fence-split. He had got the shivers, or shakes. Maybe he had got the fever, bitten by all those damn 'skeeters the night he camped down by the river. The most dangerous critter in the world, the 'skeeter', responsible for millions of deaths. After man, that was. Man, a natural born killer. But what about those horned rattlers in his bed? Plain as day. He had screamed and leaped out. And then they were gone. *Delirium tremens* it was. Not fever. He looked at his sweating, shaking palms. Too much bourbon. How could he keep steady hold of a gun? He had gone out to the drugstore and bought laudanum and quinine. Back in his room he dosed himself with a syringe. It gave him a certain relief, hitting him at the back of his neck and spreading through to his fingertips. He dressed carefully in cleanly laundered linen, his funereal suit, bowstring tie, silver-toed boots. The coughing had ceased for a spell. He went down to the saloon, took his customary corner seat. He was more in control, if a hazy dream control.

'Gimme a hot toddy of bourbon with lemon and angostura,' he called to one of the waiter girls.

'Don't you want sugar?'

142

'No, I don't.' He eyed the frilly-dressed girl, coldly, all sexual desire for such creatures long past. 'I like it bitter,' he grinned. 'Like drinking the dregs of my heart.'

'You're quite the poet.' A ruddy-faced, pig-snouted rancher and two iron-clad *hombres* had drifted over. He was a renowned cardsharp and they wanted to see him bested. 'And that's some revolver. Where'd'ja get it?'

'Used to belong to the Emperor Maximilian 'fore they put him up in front of a firing squad in '66.' Holliday's clammy fingers touched the silver and gold inlay. 'Or so I'm told. Percussion cap and ball. Had it converted by the Thuer system.' He drew it from the holster and lay it on the table. 'I allus back an ace with a gun.'

A spasm of coughing racked him, as if he would cough up his lungs. He spat bloody sputum to the sawdust floor and wiped tears from his eyes. The men watched fascinated, like they might watch some sick dog. 'Sounds like you ain't long for this world,' the pig-snout grinned.

'Maybe longer than you.' Holliday stared at him, his hair over his eyes, and eyes like twin pools of bloodstained piss. 'So just shut up and deal.'

James Casper came in, debonair as ever in jodhpurs, shiny English boots and hacking jacket. But he looked worried. Frank Canton was by his side, tall and neatly attired beneath his long riding coat, but he, too, seemed edgy. The sheriff was with them holding a sawn-off.

'Hear you been havin' a bit of trouble?' Holliday drawled, glancing up from the cards, and taking a bourbon straight this time. 'Damn fine whiskey.'

'Should be,' Casper snapped, stroking back his unruly hair. 'It's been sitting in a charred barrel for seven years. Yes, you could say we've had some trouble. My engine derailed, my line blown skyhigh, not to mention thirty-something men killed or out of action.'

'Forty men I heard, against three.' Holliday gave a hollow laugh as he flicked a card and pushed some dollars into the pot. 'So what did the brave Frank Canton do?'

'More than you sat there on your butt all day swilling best bourbon,' Casper shouted. 'When you going to earn your pay?'

'When he comes,' Holliday said. 'Make no mistake, he'll be here.'

'That man's got the luck of the devil,' Canton cried, angrily. 'We should have got him when I took his horse out from under him. If it weren't for that sniper up on the ridge, and that Injin.'

'Tut tut, poor dear.' Holliday made a chicken-clucking sound. 'Is the marshal gittin' sceered? He ain't got a gang of sixty killers to back him like he had up in Wyoming.'

'I've warned you.' Canton pointed a finger at him, and licked his lips. 'When this is finished . . .'

Holliday gave a scoffing grin and concentrated on the game. Casper asked the sheriff, 'Haven't we got any more gunmen we can hire?'

'They all seem to have suddenly discovered they got work to do out at their farms, too busy to ride with the posse. There's a few deadbeats and drifters we could rope in.'

'Get them,' Casper said, and there was a note of dog-fear pleading in his voice. 'I'll pay ten dollars a day. Get them up on the roofs of the houses. We'll cut him down if he dares come in.'

'He'll dare,' Holliday said, before he was caught with another coughing fit.

'Come on,' Casper shouted. 'Let's get organized.' He pointed at his foreman, who was cringing away behind a crowd at the bar, trying to remain unseen. 'Take a rifle, Jones, and get up in one of the rooms. Shoot to kill.'

'Oh, no, sir.' The foreman, in his torn check suit, demurred. 'Not me, sir. That man's threatened to kill me if he sees me again. I don't know nuthin' about gunfighting. I'm just a railroad man, Mister Casper. I've had enough. I'm gettin' the first train out of here.'

Frank Canton intervened, jabbing his finger into his gut. 'You get a gun and conceal yourself at a window, you fat fool, or it's I who will kill you.'

'The big I am,' Holliday sneered, snidely. 'I who will kill you. Who's he playing at, God? Why don't you fight your own battles, Canton? You're supposed to be fast, aincha?'

Canton ignored him, turning to the group at the bar. 'You men, I'm deputizing you. Go over to the sheriff's office and draw yourselves rifles and ammunition.'

The men muttered among themselves, hangdog. They downed their drinks and ambled out of the bar. They got onto their horses and rode quickly out of town. They weren't planning to be gun-fodder.

'Hey, that ain't right.' The pig-faced rancher was pointing at Doc Holliday's hand. 'Where'dja get that ace from?'

KRA-BAM! The report of the explosion made

everybody jump. The farmer staggered back, clutching his chest. He gradually expired on the floor in a pool of blood.

'Take your dead friend and get out,' Holliday ordered the other two players. 'Nobody accuses me of cheating.'

When they had dragged the corpse away, he blew lovingly down the revolver barrel, and grinned at the company. 'He was gettin' on my nerves.'

He stood and went to the bar, ordered another bottle. 'OK, let this Texan come,' he said, turning to them. 'I'm ready for him.'

*

> With one hand on my rifle,
> And the other on the horn,
> I'm the best durn cowboy
> That ever was born.

Lucy winced as she listened to Pete's caterwauling. 'Is that how you see yourself?'

'It's only a song. I gotta keep my spirits up.'

'All this rifle shooting, this killing and dynamiting, it appals me. And all you do is sing about it. Doesn't anything bother you?'

'Yeah, the pain in my knee.' He was sprawled out in the natural hollow of a hilltop where they had lit a small fire and were brewing up coffee. 'I'm sure one lucky sonuvagun. That poor damn hoss coulda broke my thigh bone. I guess it's jest kinda twisted a bit.'

'What are we going to do?'

'Me an' Henry's goin' in at sundown. We gotta finish it. You wait here.'

'No, I'm coming with you.' Her face was tense and

determined as she studied him. 'Aren't you frightened they might kill you?'

'Sure.' His face above the beard creased into laughter lines. 'A bullet's bound to git me one day. A man wouldn't be human if he weren't feared. I try not to let it bother me.'

'I ain't sittin' here all afternoon,' Howling Wolf said. 'I need to be doing something. I'll go back up to the ridge and keep watch. If you hear the raven sound – Quo! Quo! – that's me. It means they're coming.'

When the thud of hooves of Howling Wolf's stallion had echoed away, Pete finished his coffee and drawled, 'It sure is warm here in the sun outa the wind. Nice ain't it? You know the best way to relax yourself afore a fight. . .?'

'No! She looked up at him, her eyes alarmed. 'Don't be ridiculous! Nor so unflattering. You mean you want to use me to relax yourself.'

'Aw, come on, Lucy.' He reached out a hand to her. 'Don't be so prissy. You wouldn't deny a man his last request when he might be dead tomorrow?'

'Don't be absurd! Who do you think I am? *What*? In broad daylight?' She tried to suppress a smile, and her grey eyes twinkled. 'Really!' You've got a nerve.'

Howling Wolf sat up on the ridge watching the torn-up railroad track, the derailed engine, the blue vista of mountains, the distant haze of smoke of wood fires rising from the town of Sulphur Springs. He wondered how his wife was. How the schoolchildren were getting on without him. How he would fare when they went in to finish the fight. 'It's a good day to die,' he said.

There was no sign of anyone looking for them, so he returned to his horse and rode back to the hollow. On the crest he looked down and hauled in with surprise. If anyone else had seen it they might have thought it was a man and and a young cowboy. They were crouched buck-assed naked, their pants around their knees, going at it like a couple of copulating buffalo, only Miss Luffy's shirt was rumpled up, and his hands were fondling her breasts as they swung to the motion. Henry watched, bewitched, as she gave a shrill gasping groan and lowered her head, her hat going skew-whiff. Pete's hat was still in place and his face serious as he strove. It looked to be a very serious business.

'Quo! Quo!' Howling Wolf called, and rode his horse down to them. 'Well, I wouldn't have believed it of you, Miss Luffy.'

The couple on the ground froze in congress, and the girl covered her face in her arms, her posterior still high, and groaned. 'I'm sorry Henry. You chose an inopportune moment to return.'

'You sure did,' Pete growled, hanging onto her. 'Clear off. Give us ten minutes. Play the white man.'

Henry grinned and wheeled his horse away. 'Ten minutes? Sink me! You sure that will suffice, old man?'

When he had gone Pete collapsed upon her, kissing the nape of her neck.

'I've never been so embarrassed,' she said, and her body was shaking with laughter.

He caught her giggles, and brayed with laughter, too. 'Durned redskin. He's put me off my stroke!'

Fourteen

Lucy felt wild and liberated, all her inhibitions fallen from her as she rode towards Sulphur Springs. They passed the jack-knifed Katie engine and carriage, the wreckage of the van, the fly-buzzing corpses sprawled in attitudes of death, and she felt little pity. They had accepted Mammon's dollar and tried to kill her, wipe out her life's work. Pill-brained fools. A righteous anger seethed inside her. A scholar's contempt for the petty-minded money-worshippers. 'What do we do when we get there?' she shouted.

'You hold the hosses, gal.' The Texan was riding the stiff-legged pack mule, jerking along between them, the hooves beating out a staccato tattoo. 'Me an' Henry will do what we need to do.'

They loped along what remained of the winding railroad track down to the flat, Howling Wolf bare-chested, chanting his battle song, Black Pete, relaxed but determined, crooning, contrapuntally, 'Black, black, black was the colour of my true love's hair . . . her lips were something rosy fair . . . her face the saddest I did see . . . nor I can sleep when I think of thee.'

Lucy experienced a strange stab of jealousy as she glanced at him. Was he, as he rode towards death,

149

thinking of that first wife of his, uncaring about
death, wanting, perhaps, to join her across the shad-
owy valley? How different it might have been if she,
Lucy, had been his first love, and he, when he was
young and honest, before life scarred him, hers . . . .

He glanced across and smiled at her. 'Henry's one
hell of a lousy singer, ain't he? I reckon the chief
rats'll be holed up in the Wild Cat Saloon. I'm gonna
have to go in. You wait for us, but, if we don't come
out, you ride like hell, ride for your very life, and
don't stop 'til you get to Guthrie or Fort Arbuckle.
You hear?'

Lucy pulled her Stetson down over her brow and
nodded, for they had sighted the turntable on the
track, and the big locomotive, The Flyer stood facing
back north, its engine idling, about half a mile their
side of the town.

Pete drew alongside and jumped up on the foot-
plate, putting his Smith & Wesson to the engineer's
head. 'I need you to drive this thang slowly on
through the town,' he said.

Henry jumped into the rear carriage and left the
mule and stallion to Lucy's keeping as the Flyer got up
steam and began to slide out along the track. It was
going at a good lick as it passed the graveyard, and its
steam whistle moaned mournfully as the first of the
clapboard houses came into sight. Howling Wolf spotted a sniper up on the roof of the butcher's shop, with
its bloody carcases hanging outside. His arrow flew
straight and true and the gunman clutched at his
chest, and joined the dead meat down below.

There were more newly enlisted desperadoes
stationed all along Main Street: one behind the
turret of the bank, another in the window of the

ladies' millinery store, two crouched in the livery-stable loft, several on the opposite side of the street, on the roof of the gun shop, behind barrels outside the billiards hall, in the alley by the barber's shop . . . .

The Texan's Creedmore rattled out as the train moved through. He was blazing away, levering the weapon with long-practised ease, potting them like ducks, watching them tumble and fall, and seeing yet another appear, the flash and clatter of gunfire, bullets whanging off the steel of the locomotive all about him, turning to look along the other side, and noting yet another gasping his last breath as the Wichita's arrow found him.

When they passed the Wild Cat Saloon he sent a volley of rifle fire into its windows and walls. Three men who ran out firing wildly at him did a slow-motion dance of death as his lead caught them.

'Haul on the brakes,' he shouted. 'Now, let's reverse back up the street, make sure there's no other dingbats about.'

He reloaded and kept a wary eye out as the train went shushing and clanging back up the street. There appeared to be no other ambushers so he jumped lightly down, and saw Henry do likewise at his end of the two carriages. He tossed the Creedmore away and loosened the Smith & Wesson on his thigh as he slowly walked towards the Wild Cat. 'Black, black, black is the colour of my true love's hair,' he whispered.

They were waiting for him inside as he knew they would be. 'Stay outside,' he gritted out to Henry, who had his Dragoon revolver out. 'Cover the street. Do as I tell you. This is my party.'

He kicked open the batwing doors and stepped
into the gloom. His eyes weren't as good as they once
had been and took time to get accustomed. But he
had the raw red rays of the setting sun at his back and
had the advantage of anyone inside at that moment.
He heard a caustic laugh and looking along,
surprised, he saw a gangling fellow in a silk plug hat
and black frock coat sitting at a table playing cards
with himself as if none of the gunfire had happened.

'Welcome, my friend,' the card player called.
'You've frightened everybody off. They've skedad-
dled out the back way. Looks like I'm reduced to
playing solitaire.'

'Doc?' A sliver of fear entered the Texan's heart
when he recognized him. The fastest man ever to
draw a gun. Faster than a rattlesnake's strike. 'Doc
Holliday. What you doin' here?'

'I'm here to kill you,' Holliday smiled. 'Nuthin'
personal. It's just a job. Say, aren't you – yes, I remember now – Bowen, the young marshal at Dodge 'fore
me an' Wyatt took over. You did a good job. Why was
it you turned outlaw?'

'A woman with black hair,' he said. 'My wife.'
There was a rustle of movement behind the bar and
the Texan edgily spun towards it.

'Alright, boys and gals, come out from there,'
Holliday called. 'He ain't gonna hurt you.'

Several of the prairie nymphs fearfully showed
themselves, followed by the burly barkeep, his hands
raised, his face twisted into an apologetic grin. 'You
been givin' us a lot of trouble, Mr Bowen,' he said,
'but I ain't got nuthin' to do with this.'

The Texan glanced around and back to the
dentist, who was shuffling the deck. 'Pity we ain't got

time for a game, Doc,' he whispered.

'Yes, indeed it is.' Holliday slowly rose, coiled and taut as a spring. 'I suppose you're wondering where Mr Canton's got to?'

'That had crossed my mind.' The Texan took his stance in the centre of the deserted saloon, thirty paces from the gunslinger, close enough to look into his liverish eyes, eyes as cold as death, 'I'm ready when you are, Doc.'

Holliday carefully finished the bourbon in his glass, wiped his yellow moustache and threw back his frock coat to reveal the Emperor Maximilian's long-barrelled revolver hung across his loins. He showed buck-teeth in a scoffing smile. 'Now!' he shouted, and the weapon appeared to spring into his hand, scooped from the greased holster and aimed at the Texan, but, as he fired he was convulsed with coughing, his whole body in spasms of shuddering. His shot crashed out wild.

The Texan had his S. & W. out a split-second behind him, and as he pointed it at Holliday's belt buckle and squeezed the trigger he knew the dentist would have beaten him to the draw ... in better times. In a similar split-second, he diverted his aim. His slug sliced through Holliday's thigh, knocking him down.

The dentist fell back, grimacing with agony and spitting blood at the same time. Doubled up on the floor he groped for his boot pistol, with its eye-gouger attachment. Bowen was standing over him, but behind him he saw Canton on the balcony, stealthily creeping forward to aim his carbine at the Texan's back. 'Bastard!' he shouted, and squeezed the trigger.

Black Pete looked up and saw the lanky deputy marshal jerk like a puppet, drop his carbine, and topple forward, somersaulting from the balcony to crash onto a card table.

'Thanks, Doc,' he said.

'I always hated a back-shooter,' Holliday gasped out. 'If I can't get you, why should he?'

Sheriff Hank Lipcott appeared at the kitchen doorway, a 12-gauge spurting fire from both barrels. The Texan rolled to one side as buckshot peppered the walls, but as he raised himself to return fire he saw Howling Wolf's arrow was there first. Lipcott was struggling to pull it from his chest.

Lucy Luffy, in denims, leather coat and straight-brimmed hat, flitted in through the back way, her Mauser in her hand. 'Watch out!' she shouted, as she saw the fat foreman, Harry Jones, emerge from one of the curtained-off whore's cribs, his rifle aimed at the Texan on the floor. She fired and her bullet went neatly between Jones' eyes.

'Nice shootin',' Pete said, getting to his feet. 'Them li'l popguns are OK if you hit the right place.'

She lowered the gun, abjectedly. 'I was aiming at his leg.'

'Nice shootin', nonetheless, son,' Holliday cackled. 'Can one of you pass me that bourbon. My damn leg hurts like hell.'

'Where's Casper gotten to?' Howling Wolf asked.

'He's getting away!' The Eurasian girl, My Ling, had come from a bedroom door. 'He's running out on us. He's gone down the back stairs.'

There was the sound of the Flyer getting up steam, rushing at full throttle down the rails in Main Street. Pete strode to the batwing doors, his S. & W. raised, and saw James Casper sprinting across the dust, a bag in his hand, flagging the locomotive down as it rushed towards him. He was out of range of accurate revolver fire and it looked like he was going to make his escape. The engineer was looking out of the cab, ready to help him aboard, slowing to about ten miles an hour.

Casper, in a funk of fear, ran out into its path, looking behind him as Pete's shot crashed out and spat into the dust by his feet. He ducked down with alarm, and, as he did so, tripped, and sprawled over the rail. The engineer stared in horror and slammed on the brakes, but there was no way he could stop. There was a grinding, flashing, screeching of locked wheels, and a scream as Casper looked up, a second before they crushed his skull like an egg shell, but a shell that oozed scarlet blood.

The Texan strolled over, took a look at him, at the burst open bag from which dollar notes were fluttering away on the breeze. He shrugged, and glanced up at the engineer. 'Guess your boss lost his head,' he said.

'When you've cleaned up that mess you better head for Guthrie. Tell the coroner and chief marshal to get down here. There's a lot of explaining to be done.'

He went to pick up his Creedmore and ambled back to the Wild Cat Saloon. 'How's it going, Doc?' he asked.

'Aw, it's only a flesh wound,' the gambler grinned, patting My Ling on the head. 'This young lady's giving me first aid.'

'Pass me that bourbon. I need a slug.' The Texan sat down, picked up the pack and began to deal, passing the bottle to Howling Wolf. 'What's it to be? Aces high?' He glanced over at the girl. 'Fancy a hand, Lucy?'

'Sure,' she smiled. 'Why not?'

Fifteen

The poker game had lasted all night. They had put the thousands of dollars in Casper's bag – that which hadn't blown away on the wind – and Frank Canton's hefty wad into the pot. Inevitably the Texan lost. 'I don't know how you do it,' he growled, as he got to his feet. 'You're one crafty ole fox.'

Doc grinned as he scooped the winnings into his carpet bag. 'This'll keep me in bourbon up in that sanitarium. Medical bills is sky high.'

'So long,' the Texan called to Henry, who, with his arm around Judy and the children, stood proudly in front of the log cabin museum in Tishomingo. 'Take care of them bones.'

On his old grey mare he set off past the cotton mill and tall tobacco warehouses, the piles of produce waiting shipment down river, the 'civilized' stores and cabins of the Chickasaws. He was sorry to leave their land, a verdant one of woods and pastures, waterfalls and sulphur springs, lakes and clear rivers, salt slicks and quail meadows, blackjack hills and dogwood trails where fish and game abounded. Land grants to the railroads would drive wedges into the

157

old ways, bringing change, and white settlers would soon be infiltrating.

He was surprised to meet a wagon driven by the beady-eyed Milt Freeman lumbering along a precipitous trail. Pete levelled his revolver and called, 'Where you think you're going?'

'I don't want no trouble,' Freeman whined. 'I'm just a newspaperman. I'm getting out. I'll start again in Texas.'

'A rat deserting the sinking ship.' He took a look in the canvas-covered back. There was the heavy iron Washington hand press, the inks, rolls of newsprint, typefaces, all the rigmarole. He kneed the mare back up to the front. 'Git down from that box.'

Freeman did so, trembling. 'You wouldn't shoot me?'

'You were the cause of all that trouble. You an' that Casper. All them men killed because of what . . . your damned lies.'

'I was only printing what I was told. I thought—'

'You libelled a fine woman.' The Texan slashed away the harness of the wagon horses, sent them cantering away. He fired off a shot to keep them going. 'Take your clothes off?'

'What?'

'Everything. Your boots, the lot. Hurry it up. Or you want to go with this lot?' When the man was stark naked, he picked up his belongings, tossed them into the wagon. 'See you've still got a dandruff problem,' he said, flicking his fingers. 'Put your shoulder to that wagon. Go on.' He backed the mare up to the tailboard and helped him heave.

The wagon rolled forward and tumbled over the sheer precipice, bouncing and rolling, smashing on the rocks far below.

'Now git. Go on. Clear out, you lousy so-called reporter trash.' He fired shots at the man's feet and watched him go dancing and running away, a pale and scrawny bag of bones. 'Give 'em my love in Texas.'

Lucy Luffy was in her dove-grey dress, her hair piled up on top, wire spectacles on the tip of her *retroussé* nose. She was studying paintings on a cliff wall depicting masked and tattooed dancers, gods and people. All around her at the new digging site Indian workers were carefully scraping away earth. 'These are amazing,' she said. 'We have found some exquisite pottery. And look at this intricately carved bone gorgette. There was a sophisticated civilization here a thousand years ago. There could be a maze of underground chambers.'

'Yeah? How did the inquest go?' he asked, changing the subject.

'Oh, My Ling testified that she heard Casper plotting to kill us all, you, me and Henry. Freeman admitted his story was lies, printed an apology.'

'Yeah, I met him.'

'I had an account of the true facts sent to the *New York Times*. It should help raise funds for our work. They found Dr Stares' coffin floating on a river. They had neglected to bore holes in it so it came to the top. Apparently young Casper had always been a bad lot. His father's agreed to divert the railroad. So everything turned out OK. I do believe this is going to be one of the most important sites in the country.'

He watched her as she daintily touched the ochre murals. She was in another world, a world of her own. 'By the way,' she said, 'I sent the balance of your payment to your son. I thought he might make better use of it.'

'That's mighty fine.' He touched her waist and kissed her cheek. 'Keep up the good work.'

She looked up at him and her smile was no longer tight-lipped but wide and dimpled. 'You know, you taught me – I'm not sure what – but something. I'm grateful. I'll miss you.'

He climbed on the bronc, touched his hat to her, and glanced up at the darkening sky as thunder rumbled.

'I tol' ya the weather was fit to change. You better git them finds under canvas. Take care now.'

'And you, too,' she called, as she watched him ride off back towards the Chisholm Trail, 'you old war horse.' ✗ IV

AUTHOR'S NOTE

For the purpose of dramatic construction the timescale of historical events, and the life span of certain real-life characters, has been telescoped in this fiction.

P